"Tell Me ... Luke Said Tightly.

"I don't want to hurt you any more than I have."

But Brenna couldn't do that, any more than she could tell her heart to stop aching for him. She looked boldly into his face. Even in the dark she could read the hunger there. Lightning lit the room for one silvery instant, and Luke's eyes blazed with unconcealed need.

"Brenna," he groaned, investing her name with all the pain and longing they'd known in the past ten years. Her name was on his lips, and then his lips were on her skin.

The storm drew closer, and a gust of cool wind blew open the front door, rattling the screen against the frame. The air rushed over them with the fury of demon breath, but they were lost in each other's passion, their own storm rivaling anything outside.

Luke McShane was a dream lover, come to possess Brenna with the past.

Dear Reader:

Welcome to Silhouette Desire—sensual, compelling, believable love stories written by and for today's woman. When you open the pages of a Silhouette Desire, you open yourself up to a whole new world— a world of promising passion and endless love.

Each and every Silhouette Desire is a wonderful love story that is both sensuous *and* emotional. You're with the hero and heroine each and every step of the way—from their first meeting, to their first kiss...to their happy ending. You'll experience all the deep joys—and occasional tribulations—of falling in love.

This month, look for *Candlelight for Two* by Annette Broadrick, which is the highly anticipated sequel to *A Loving Spirit*. And don't miss Kathleen Korbel's terrific *Man of the Month*, *Hotshot*. Of course, I think every July Silhouette Desire is a winner!

So enjoy...

Lucia Macro
Senior Editor

KELLY JAMISON

ECHOES FROM THE HEART

SILHOUETTE *Desire*

Published by Silhouette Books New York

America's Publisher of Contemporary Romance

SILHOUETTE BOOKS
300 East 42nd St., New York, N.Y. 10017

ISBN: 0-373-05579-X

First Silhouette Books printing July 1990

Printed in the U.S.A.

KELLY JAMISON

grew up in a small town and often makes rural communities the settings for her books. She always knew that she wanted to be a writer. After graduating from college, she worked for a newspaper that was so tiny it didn't even have its own camera. Whenever they needed to take a picture, they'd borrow a camera from the woman next door!

Kelly is a rabid chocoholic and pizza addict, who also paints in watercolors and rides her bike. She has written as Kelly Adams.

One

─────

A silver wind means a big storm, Brenna McShane thought as she brushed back a lock of shoulder-length, red-gold hair that the wind insisted on flinging into her face. She glanced up at the gray clouds scuttling across the sky, then slid into her car and turned the key, sighing as the ignition clicked and remained silent.

The solenoid was bad, her brother Joe had told her. Brenna waited a minute, then tried the key again. This time the engine coughed to life and she pulled away from the curb in front of the Chestnut Tree Cafe and headed home.

Stately maples lined the main highway through the heart of Waldo, Illinois, and the blustery wind ruffled the leaves, turning up their silvery undersides and making the trees look like enormous coquettes trying to hold down their petticoats. Of course there was no such thing in scientific literature as a silver wind, but Brenna's father had called it that when she was a child and, sure enough, it always brought a big rain. This June was particularly dry and hot, and a big rain would be welcome, Brenna thought as she drove out of town past parched cornfields and stunted soybeans.

Brenna was tired this evening but all keyed up, too, a combination that she attributed to the weather. It was almost as if she expected something more than the storm, something to ride into town on the wind and turn things upside down, the way the breeze was flipping the garbage cans at the farmhouse she was passing now, sending them rolling noisily across the yard.

For an instant Brenna was tempted to pull the car over and run alongside the fence the way she had as a child, but she squelched the idea immediately. She just wasn't the kind of woman who got out of a car—however minimally her vehicle qualified as a car—and raced the wind.

Brenna was sole owner of the Chestnut Tree Cafe. She was also chief cook, aided by her Aunt Loraine and a onetime drifter named Fergie Henderson. The café was opened in 1950 by Brenna's grandfather, who served hearty breakfasts, burgers and fries and an evening blue-plate special. The café took its name from the enormous chestnut tree that grew in the front yard. A blight killed the tree the next year, but it didn't matter because when the new highway came through, it lopped off the yard anyway. Prices had gone up somewhat over the years, and now there were bran muffins on the breakfast menu—Fergie was a firm believer in fiber—but the original knotty-pine paneling was still on the walls and the placemats were plain white, the way they'd always been. And that was fine for the town of Waldo.

Waldo, Illinois, did not take to change easily, and neither did Brenna McShane.

A quarter mile later Brenna slowed and turned right into her own driveway. She and Luke had bought the plain-white clapboard house with its green shutters right after they were married, their heads filled with plans for planting an apple orchard in the back pasture and setting tulips around the brand-new gleaming white mailbox on which they'd so carefully painted McShane in bold black letters. Brenna checked the mailbox—empty—then drove toward the house.

There were only four apple trees left in the pasture, obviously of hardy stock to have survived the years of neglect. And the name on the mailbox was barely legible now, almost ten years after the divorce. The long driveway swallowed up gravel the way a black hole gobbles light; the only things keeping the parallel ruts from joining forces and becoming one big gully were the dandelions and foxtails in between. The garage remained open all the time because the door had come off its track and no longer closed.

The house was no great beauty, either, Brenna noted glumly as she stopped the car. Paint blistered and peeled all over, like a fat matron who had fallen asleep sunbathing at the beach. Two of the shutters had fallen off, and Brenna had stuck them in the garage. Two more swung and banged when there was wind like today. The door no longer locked, and there was a man on a stepladder hammering her shutter.

There was a man on a stepladder hammering her shutter.

Cautiously Brenna got out of the car. If it was Frank Hargrove, she was just going to have to be firm and tell him she wasn't buying any more insurance from him, no matter how many little chores he did for her.

Brenna shut the car door, folded her arms across her chest and frowned at the man's back. The wind continued whipping her hair around her face and she cursed herself for not letting Loraine talk her into going to Loretta at the Clip 'N Curl for a cut and perm. She'd always worn her hair long and straight, and she was probably too old at twenty-nine to keep doing it. Her pink-and-white-print skirt was full and it blew up above her knees. Brenna hastened to push it down, all the while staring at the stranger's back. His jet-black hair was slightly shaggy and the wind ruffled it caressingly, making Brenna wonder how it would look after a woman's fingers had sifted through it. Odd she should think of that. She cleared her throat pointedly, but he continued hammering, apparently not hearing her over the wind and the methodical thumps of hammer meeting nail.

She watched the muscles move rhythmically beneath the straining fabric of his light blue work shirt and when he stepped down the ladder, his jeans emphasized lean hips and muscular legs. Brenna adjusted the straps of her pink tank top, tapped the toe of one sensibly comfortable shoe on the rutted drive and cleared her throat again, louder.

He took his time about turning around. When he finally did, the breath went out of her as if she'd been kicked. All she could think of was that her silver wind had indeed blown up a storm this time.

Standing on her porch with his legs apart, hammer in hand, dazzling blue eyes almost daring her to come closer, stood all six feet three inches of Brenna's ex-husband, Luke McShane, ten years older and ten times handsomer than she remembered. Those blue eyes met her brown ones and immediately they clashed.

"Hello, Brenna," he said softly. The words seemed to touch her mouth as though he had suddenly closed the distance between them and kissed her.

Unconsciously she raised two fingers to her lips and brushed away the piece of hair clinging there. "What are you doing here, Luke?"

He laughed wryly and tossed the hammer down. It landed with a loud clang, making Brenna jump.

"I didn't think I needed an invitation to come back to the town where I grew up," he said, eyes appraising her. "I've been back often enough in the last few years."

"But not here," she reminded him. "Not at this house." *And not to see me.*

"I would have come," he said hesitantly, his eyes never leaving her face, "if I'd thought I was welcome."

She didn't have an answer for that, so they stood there and stared at each other. There was just a hint of gray at Luke's temples to remind her that he was thirty now and that this tension between them existed only in her mind. The marriage was long gone and what she felt for this man was only a lingering anger for what might have been and never was. And pain for what had hurt them both.

"I need to wash up," he announced finally.

Making him stand on the porch was silly, Brenna told herself. He'd once lived in this house with her. There was no reason he couldn't come inside long enough to wash his hands.

Only with Luke, things had a way of not going the way you expected. She had a feeling that inviting him inside would only be the beginning of her troubles. With Luke she had learned to expect the unexpected.

Feigning nonchalance, she shrugged. "You know where the bathroom is."

But he stood where he was until she mounted the steps, and then he fell in behind her as she opened the door. She wouldn't look at him—those searching blue eyes had scorched themselves onto her mind's eye the instant she'd recognized him—but she could feel his presence, as electrifying as the distant lightning that sizzled across the fields. The wind gusted and caught the screen door, slamming it against the house. Luke caught it and closed it again.

They left the heavy wooden door open and Brenna welcomed the rush of fresh air at her back as she made her way to the kitchen. She was suddenly aware of how familiar and yet how aged everything in the house must appear to Luke. It struck her that this was the kind of house where grandmothers were supposed to live. The living room with its worn wooden floors burnished to a glossy shine, upholstered furniture that sagged in the middle and trailed tired springs like hernias, sedate lace curtains over pull-down shades that were slightly yellowed from the sun and the ancient wallpaper were all the furnishings one associated with someone much older than Brenna, someone who spent her days knitting afghans—like the blue-and-white one on the back of the chair—and baking chocolate-chip cookies for grandchildren. Only there weren't any grandchildren. Or even children.

Brenna suddenly wanted to fling a heavy dropcloth over everything in the living room to keep Luke from looking at it. She glanced warily at him and saw him looking at the pressed violets mounted in a walnut frame over the rocking chair. She wondered how she had come to be here like this with her ex-husband, living this life and waiting for…what?

She got ice from the freezer and the pitcher of cold tea. All the while she was pouring the tea she could hear him washing his hands in the bathroom down the hall, and she could see lightning streaking from one gray cloud to another outside her kitchen window.

"The sink leaks," he said from the doorway. She put the glasses on the tiny table and straightened to stare at him.

"And the tub needs new caulking, the ceiling has a water stain and two tiles are broken," she reiterated tonelessly, as if to say, *so what.*

He walked to the table and for the first time Brenna noticed his limp. A racing accident? she wondered briefly. He sat down wearily and leaned back, eyeing her as he took a deep gulp of tea. Her spine still stiff, Brenna sat down and studied the table as she drank her own tea.

"Things need taking care of around here," he said quietly.

"Things have been getting along just fine for the last ten years," she said, still not looking at him. She'd forgotten that distinctly male rasp to his voice. Luke McShane had always looked and sounded as though he'd just climbed out of some reckless female's bed, and Brenna's stomach muscles clenched at the memory of that voice on the mornings he'd climbed out of hers.

"What are you doing buying insurance from Frank Hargrove again?" he asked abruptly, reaching into his pocket and shoving a pile of letters onto the table.

"That's my mail!" she cried, reaching for it. Her hand briefly encountered his and she jerked her fingers away as though they'd been burned. The action wasn't wasted on Luke, she noted as his jaw clenched. Something flared in his eyes and then died.

"I told you ten years ago that Hargrove oversells," he insisted, flicking the bill toward her with one long, tanned finger. "The man would insure a housefly in a swatter factory if he thought there was a commission in it."

"I own a business," Brenna said pointedly, aggravated by his nosiness and his assumption that he still had any say in her life. "I need a lot of insurance."

Luke snorted. "He's probably got you covered for cakes that fail to rise and burned biscuits. And what's this reminder that it's time to get your oil changed at Harvey's Quick Shop? I can change your oil in five minutes."

"Unfortunately you don't pop in every five thousand miles," Brenna reminded him mildly.

He ignored that and went on leafing through her mail.

"Your order's in at the Penney's catalog center," he informed her, holding up another postcard. "New pots and pans?"

"A nightgown," she said and immediately regretted telling him because he was looking definitely interested.

"Flannel?" he said, hazarding a guess, sounding as though he hoped she'd say his guess was wrong.

"Could be," she said noncommittally.

Luke shook his head. "I always liked you in those little short lacy things with the thin straps, but you never listened. And while we're on the subject of clothing, who the hell owns those socks in the bathroom?"

Brenna frowned until she remembered she'd been cleaning out a dresser drawer yesterday and had come across some old knee-highs she used to wear when she went walking in the winter. She'd used them to dust the window ledges, then washed them out and threw them over the shower rod.

"A traveling salesman," she said dryly. "I do his underwear whenever he comes through town."

"You never hung my socks over the shower rod," Luke said, managing to sound wounded that he hadn't rated this personal touch.

"That's because I had a working clothes dryer at the time," she told him, immediately regretting it when she saw the triumphant light in his eyes.

"So that doesn't work, either," he said, shaking his head. "It's almost new."

"It's ten years old," she told him pointedly.

"Yeah, I guess it is," he said at last, looking sad and tired all at once. "Brenna, I know it's none of my business—"

"No, it's not," she broke in. "How I live now is no concern of yours, Luke. That changed a long time ago."

Thunder rumbled overhead and rain began lashing the window in sheets. Brenna got up and hurried into the living room to close the front door. When she got back to the kitchen, Luke was rummaging in the refrigerator, setting cheese and mustard on the counter. The set of his head and the way his arms moved with brisk efficiency were so familiar and so buried in her memories that she felt tears sting her eyes. So many times she'd awakened in the middle of the night, dreaming that his arms went around her, that his mouth sought the nape of her neck the way it used to. But that was long past now. What had happened ten years ago had torn them so far apart that they might as well be strangers. So much pain. And it had never gone away.

"What do you want?" she said sharply, the cry in her voice making him turn around.

"I was making a sandwich," he said hesitantly.

"No, I mean here. What do you want here?" She had to know. She had to know so she could keep the old pain at bay until he was gone again. How many hours, how many days did she have to get through?

Slowly he set the bologna on the counter and shut the refrigerator door. "Brenna," he said softly, coming toward her.

She stood in the doorway nearly trembling, terrified he would touch her and that such overwhelming feelings would come tumbling back that she would begin crying. He stopped a foot away and she was struck again by the sorrow in his eyes. A handsome man with such a devilish curve to his mouth should never be sad, she thought in distraction. And yet they both carried such a painful burden.

Ten years old. Their daughter would have been almost ten. But now there was no daughter, no laughter, no love. Their baby had been stillborn ten years ago next month. And the marriage had been torn irreparably. Like lace trying to support a heavy weight, it had ripped in two, sending Luke and Brenna reeling in opposite directions.

"Your leg," she said hoarsely, her eyes locked with his unfathomable blue ones. "You hurt it."

Some expression flitted across his face and then was gone. He shrugged. "Nothing major."

He didn't elaborate and Brenna sensed a reluctance, some secret he was keeping from her. She wondered if he'd been racing. She couldn't imagine Luke not involved in the stock-car circuit. It would drive him crazy not to be able to clutch a steering wheel in his hands, surrounded by a mass of welded steel as he flew around the track. That had been part of their problem, the stock-car circuit. Luke had worked at an auto-body shop during the week and then on weekends from spring through fall he was gone, traveling from one race to another on the NASCAR Winston Racing Series. He competed in the late-model class, an expensive class that demanded time and money. They hadn't managed to build any lines of communication between them. The fragile threads that held them together had broken all too easily.

"Denny always said you were the fastest driver around," she said, remembering how her younger brother idolized Luke and followed in his racing footsteps. "I haven't seen him in five months now. I don't know where he is."

"He's in Iowa," Luke said.

It surprised Brenna that he kept up with Denny, and he must have read her expression because he said, "We were at the same track. He got a job with one of the promoters."

"Is he . . . doing all right?"

"I think he's getting over his divorce, if that's what you mean. And he's stopped drinking himself into oblivion every night," Luke added cautiously. He leaned one shoulder against the doorjamb and Brenna took a step back, physically and emotionally.

He hadn't really told her how Denny was. She, her older brother Joe and their father had been worried sick about Denny the last few months.

"The racing circuit is hard on marriages," she observed, sorry she'd said it as soon as the words were out.

But Luke didn't flinch. "Yeah, it is," he said quietly.

He had left after the baby was born. She had seen the pain in his eyes and the need—always the need—to escape it by racing around a circular track. He had said he was going to Iowa for one race. He said he had to get away, that he could get over it if he could just lose himself in the speed and the precise control of the track. He said he'd be back.

But Brenna knew he wouldn't return. Whatever Luke found at the track was pulling him too strongly for her to hold on to him. And so she had let Clinton Burgess, an old school friend, and his parents take her away with them to their Ozark Mountain cabin. They were gone a month and when she came back there was a letter from Luke wanting her to come to Iowa. She had torn it up and thrown it away. Two months later she filed for divorce.

The marriage had been a mistake, she told herself. She and Luke were too different. But, oh, he had been so exciting when she first met him. He was a year ahead of her in school and she was the first and only girl he asked out on a date. He was a wild, irrepressible half boy, half man with a quick sense of humor and a streak of shyness that had surprised and touched her.

The night they became lovers under the giant elm tree, swaddled in a million stars above, Brenna conceived their daughter. Luke wanted to marry her as soon as she told him about the pregnancy, and so they started their brief sojourn as husband and wife. Less than a year later, their child died before drawing breath in this world, and it was all over.

"Luke, what are you doing here?" she asked now.

"Dad's sick," he said, frowning and looking off toward the window. "He's in the hospital, and I ... need to be near him."

"Why didn't you tell me he's in the hospital?" she accused him. She'd always been fond of James McShane and she had visited him frequently since the divorce. She had visited him two weeks ago, in fact, and, concerned about his grayish pallor, had cautiously asked if he was feeling well. A lingering case of winter flu, James had said.

"He was admitted just a few days ago," Luke said, still not quite meeting her eyes. "I didn't really have ... time to call you before I came to town."

"Is he very sick?" Brenna asked hesitantly.

"It's serious," he said. "They're running tests." He shrugged helplessly. "You know Dad. He minimizes everything. He acts like it's just a cold." Luke looked clearly uncomfortable as he finally met her eyes, and Brenna could almost see the want he must be so carefully holding inside. "Brenna, I wondered if I could ... stay here awhile. While Dad's in the hospital."

"But what about his apartment?" she asked, frowning. "Couldn't you stay there?"

He shook his head. "He let it go. He was just about to move up near his brother in Minnesota when he got sick."

"Oh." She hadn't expected this. She had supposed she would see Luke again one day after the divorce, but in her imagination she had always answered her door, said "Hello, Luke" without a trace of emotion and then told him to go away and leave her alone. Now that he actually stood a heartbeat away from her, asking if he could stay in this house with her again, now that she could smell the musky male scent that was his and see the loneliness in his blue eyes, now that she could feel the heat emanating from his body, she couldn't seem to tell him to go away. And in her heart she knew she would let him stay, even if only for James's sake.

They stood there looking at each other and Brenna's heartbeat was as violent as the rain pounding the windows. The storm had brought an early nightfall, and now only the dim kitchen-ceiling light shone on the planes of Luke's face. His nose had been broken once in a fight at the track, and now there was just the tiniest crookedness to it. His high cheeks were ruddy from his time in the sun and though his mouth had that familiar quirk, there was no laughter in his expression.

Luke watched her make up her mind. He knew what she was thinking—she didn't want him here, but she had no graceful way of telling him to go. She had the same beautiful reddish-gold hair he remembered so well. But her brown eyes were darker and haunted, as though they'd seen something that had marked them forever. Quite suddenly he wanted to touch her, to assure himself that she was all right. He had thought about her often all these years, had wondered how she was getting along, but he had decided that since Brenna had filed for the divorce and wanted him out of her life permanently, then he would give her that at least.

He had told himself he would see her again, and if she told him he couldn't stay here, then he would find someplace else. But now, looking at her, seeing how fragile she was, he wanted desperately to stay here and be near her, to rest awhile and maybe fix up the house a bit. He didn't fully understand what he was feeling, but it wasn't unlike nearing the end of a journey.

Brenna met his gaze warily. She would spend a lot of time at the café, she reasoned. She needn't be around Luke that much. She could handle this.

"All right," she said at last, the hint of a quaver in her voice. "I guess you could sleep in the upstairs guest room."

"Thanks, Bren," he said quietly.

Things could be normal between them, she told herself. They were divorced now and they could find some middle ground between being friends and strangers, some neutral place where they could put the past where it belonged—in the past.

She believed that all of ten seconds. Then while rogue blue eyes studied her face, a long, lean finger that seemed to carry the heat of a thousand suns reached out to stroke her cheek. He was gently pushing back a strand of red-gold hair curled shell-like in front of her ear, but he might as well have reached for her heart. Brenna's breath came in shallow bursts as she stared up at him.

His eyes darkened subtly and a new expression entered them. They looked fierce, and yet it was a fierceness Brenna had known before, a kindling flame that had burned for her once years ago. His other hand cradled her head, his thumbs gliding in a pattern over her jaw. Luke's body had the power of a hundred hypnotists where Brenna was concerned, and she felt her blood gathering to answer this man's beck and call.

"I'd forgotten how beautiful your hair is," he murmured, his hands tugging her closer, his mouth moving restlessly over her hair. He turned his face to rub his cheek against her hair and then his mouth moved quite slowly to her own.

Time became something fluid and languid, wrapping them in its cocoon. And then it seemed to catch fire as Luke's lips traveled over Brenna's, seeking, teasing, tasting. She had never managed to will herself into a stone statue under Luke's touch, and she was no more successful this time. Her hands found his shoulders and then wound behind his back. Her eyes closed heavily and her mouth opened under his tender assault. *Luke*. It felt like aeons since that firm mouth had taken hers with the kind of passion that could make a woman forget the term lady. It was Luke who had asked her never to cut her hair because it gave him so much pleasure to run his fingers through it and bury his face there. It was Luke who had taught her the infinite small joys that made up lovemaking. Luke who had awakened her body and her heart.

His hand slid up inside the tank top until his fingers were caressing a small, firm breast. Brenna gave a gasp of pleasure that was lost in the male mouth still locked to her own. He held her tightly against him, as though the last ten years had never existed, as though he was still her husband and lover.

"Remember when I won the regional championship?" he said softly, raising his mouth long enough to ask the question.

She nodded, a fleeting smile touching her mouth. "You almost dropped the trophy trying to carry it and me upstairs at the same time."

"Better I dropped it than you," he growled huskily before his mouth descended on hers again. He moved his head, laying his rough jaw against her cheek.

"It was raining that night," she said, her voice a throaty whisper as memories flooded back. "Someone had poured a beer over your head to celebrate and you smelled like a brewery."

"And you made me get in the shower," he said. "And a few minutes later..."

She turned her head slightly and met his broadening grin. She had joined him in the shower that night, and they had ended up making love with the water cascading over them, their bodies slick and shiny under the spray. She had teased him afterward, saying the trophy was really in honor of his lovemaking that night. He had hung her flimsy silk teddy over it in the morning, and there it had stayed for a week.

The teddy had been a gift from Luke, who had shaken his head and clucked mournfully the first time he saw her usual sleeping attire—an oversize flannel shirt. And Brenna had felt different in the teddy, as though through Luke's attentive caresses and admiring glances she had somehow been transformed into a desirable, beautiful woman, someone far more sexy than her ordinary, everyday self. She was a slender, graceful woman, and it was true that her hair had caught more than one man's passing fancy. But still she felt there was nothing remarkable about her slightly bowed mouth or her frank, wide brown eyes or her sprinkling of freckles. Nothing remarkable, that is, until Luke McShane had looked at her with his lips quirked in that amused, playful tilt.

"You know, I ran across that trophy on a shelf in the garage today." He ran a hand through his hair. "That old garage could really use some sprucing up. I found some paint cans there when I got the ladder."

"No, Luke," she said, drawing away from him.

"What's wrong?" he asked, frowning.

"Nothing. Just no." He was pretending he might stay this time, and Brenna knew better than to trust Luke McShane to stay anywhere very long before he ached to be somewhere else. Another race would come along, another summer day, and he'd be off.

"Brenna, the place could use some work." He stood there, staring at her helplessly as she crossed her arms.

"Yes, it could," she agreed sharply. "But I don't want you doing it."

"Why not?" His voice took on a note of stubbornness.

"You should know why. Because it's over between us, Luke, and on the day you go driving away from here I don't want to be standing in the window crying because you're leaving. I won't let myself get used to having you around again, Luke. When you go, there won't be any regrets between us."

He took a long, deep breath and held it a moment before expelling it harshly. "I didn't come back to hurt you, Brenna."

"I'm sure you *never* meant to hurt me," she said, wanting to take the words back the instant she saw pain flood his eyes.

"No," he agreed softly. "I never did." He turned away before Brenna could soften what she'd said, and her heart ached as she watched him cross the kitchen with that slight limp and begin fixing his sandwich, carefully keeping his back to her.

She sighed and went to the sink to pour out her iced tea. The rain had slackened, and through the steady drizzle she could see Luke's car parked next to the garage. Luke had never been able to just go out and buy a car and drive it, she thought, looking at the obviously new paint job—bright red—and the carefully applied racing stripes. The car might be an older model, but Luke's touch was everywhere. He had been restoring a car three days after the baby was born. Brenna had wandered out to the garage, too lonely and sad to stay in the house, and she had seen him buffing the hood in the light filtering through the dusty windows. He didn't know she was standing in the doorway, and he was talking softly to himself, a quiet, slow, sad monologue. Brenna had caught the words *grave*, and *minister*, and the baby's name, Dory, their nickname for Dorothy. Tears had filled her eyes, and she had turned and gone blindly back to the house.

Luke had never been able to talk to her about the baby the way he was talking to himself as he worked, and that had compounded her grief immeasurably. She had felt a dark, leaden curtain descend on her heart and it hadn't lifted, even after Luke left.

Now she felt a familiar ache as she watched him move about the small kitchen. She fixed herself a sandwich after he was done, and they sat silently at the table.

He helped her wash up their two dishes, still without speaking, the two of them moving in tandem the way they used to clean up after supper. But the old lighthearted banter of ten years ago was gone. They were no longer husband and wife; they were two mourners still grieving in separate prison cells, locked inside themselves. Outside the rain fell relentlessly and Brenna thought there wasn't enough rain in the world to fill up the emptiness inside her.

She was bone weary by the time they were done, and she filled the coffee maker for the morning and started for the stairs. "I think I'll go to bed," she said without looking at him. "There are clean sheets on the bed in—in the room at the end of the hall, if you want to sleep there." The room at the end of the hall used to be their bedroom because it was the largest and it had an airy southern exposure overlooking what was to have become the apple orchard. Now Brenna used it for a guest room.

"Thanks, Brenna," he said quietly from behind her. "Go ahead and use the upstairs bathroom. I'll clean up in the one down here."

She nodded and climbed the stairs. At the top she stopped and listened to the rain hitting the roof, her eyes sliding unconsciously to the little room at the right, the room that was painted bright yellow with a cheery duck-patterned wallpaper border at the top. It would have been Dory's room. Now it sat silent and dusty, a grim reminder of the frailty of human life.

Brenna sighed and glanced over her shoulder. Luke was still standing at the foot of the stairs and his eyes were fixed on the room, too. The grief and pain on his face were almost more than she could bear. She turned away, knowing that for the first time in years she would cry herself to sleep tonight.

Two

The rain trickled to an end sometime in the morning, and when Brenna woke up she could hear it dripping steadily from the gutters, hitting the downspout with a hollow ping. Sunday was the one morning the Chestnut Tree Cafe was closed, the morning Brenna could sleep late.

She rolled over and dozed off, but a steady clanking noise woke her again. Frowning, she glanced at the clock: *7:00 a.m.* Who on God's green earth was clanking around at seven on a Sunday morning?

Luke, of course, she thought wryly as she pulled aside the curtain and looked out. She abruptly reached full wakefulness as she realized that it was her car he was clanking on. If he converted it to four-on-the-floor with dual carburetors she was going to throttle him with her bare hands. She was about to fling open the window and yell at him, but his head was buried inside the open hood. He wouldn't hear her over the racket he was creating as he tinkered with the engine, making it roar, then cutting it out.

And that pretty much summed up her experiences with Luke McShane, Brenna thought wearily as she climbed out of bed. Things went along like one of his souped-up engines, either roaring or cutting out completely.

As long as she was up this early she might as well start a batch of cinnamon rolls, she decided, pulling on her short red terry robe. They were Clinton's favorite, and she'd told him she'd bring some by today.

Two hours later the rolls were on their final rising and Brenna was standing at the window with her third cup of coffee, frowning at the mess Luke was making in her driveway. Littering the ground was an assortment of wrenches and rags. Luke was still hunched over the engine, intent on some new crime he was perpetrating there.

Brenna glanced up as she heard the purr of a new car motor during one of the rare moments when Luke wasn't racing her own engine. Lord, she thought. This was just what she needed. Clinton Burgess was driving up to her house in his brand-new four-door sedan.

Brenna sighed as Clinton got out of his car very slowly and stood staring at Luke. Finally Luke laid down his wrench and straightened, eyeing Clinton silently. A few frosty words were exchanged, if Brenna was sizing up the situation accurately, and then Clinton strode purposefully toward the house while Luke wiped his hands on a rag and stared after him.

"What's he doing here?" Clinton demanded the minute he was inside the door.

"Nice to see you, Clinton," Brenna said quietly.

Clinton ran his palm over his head, a habit he had had as long as Brenna had known him and which at the moment struck her as rather silly. His light blond hair was thinning rapidly on top, but he stubbornly moussed what he had, possibly to keep it from falling out, she thought.

Brenna leaned against the sink and crossed her arms, waiting for Clinton to unload his grievance. He had always prided himself on holding his emotions in check, and

Brenna knew he would be as fastidious in airing his complaint as he must have been in folding the white handkerchief that peeked elegantly from the pocket of his gray pinstriped suit.

"Brenna, that's *Luke*," he said at last, as though he were announcing that there was a toxic substance in her driveway.

"I know, Clinton," she said. "His father's sick."

"That doesn't excuse his coming here," he insisted. "The man left you at a very crucial time in your life. He has no business showing up here again." He shook his head with the stiff-necked style he had, a style Brenna supposed was intended to keep his hair in place. "No, no. I can't abide this."

"Clinton, you don't have to abide anything," Brenna told him wearily. "This is between Luke and me."

"I'm your friend, Brenna," he insisted, clearly wounded. "I only want what's best for you."

"And don't you think I can decide that for myself?" she asked, getting her answer as he frowned and stared at the floor.

The screen door banged on the back porch and Luke stomped up the steps to the kitchen, calling, "I need to change your fuel filter, Brenna. I have to go by the auto-parts store to pick one up." He stopped inside the kitchen door, eyeing them both warily.

"You have no business working on her car!" Clinton burst out.

"Yeah?" Luke said, wiping his hands on the rag again. "Looks like somebody ought to be working on it before it starts dropping spark plugs and belts all over the highway."

"I can have one of my mechanics at the dealership work on it anytime," Clinton insisted, turning to Brenna for confirmation.

"This is silly," she said. "If you're both so taken with my car, you can drive off in it together and leave me out of this."

Luke snorted. "It wouldn't last half a mile in the condition it's in. I bet the oil hadn't been changed in twenty thousand miles."

"I personally inspected that car two months ago," Clinton said, really agitated now. "And I offered Brenna one thousand down on a new one."

"Well, that's different," Luke said sarcastically. "The auto king of Waldo inspected my wife's car, so it must be okay."

"She's not your wife anymore, McShane!" Clinton shouted. "And I think you ought to get out of here right now."

Luke took a step forward and Brenna quickly pushed herself away from the sink. "Enough!" she said loudly, holding up a hand. "If you want to fight over my car, I'll gladly sell it to the highest bidder. But if anybody's going to tell anyone to get out of my house, then it's going to be me. And right now I'm tired of listening to the two of you bicker. You can both leave for all I care." She took a deep, angry breath, glaring at Clinton and then Luke.

Slowly Clinton ran his palm over his hair. "Well, I've got to get going," he said finally, sounding as though he'd folded up his emotions and tucked them in at the corners, like a well-made bed. "I've got an insurance agent I have to meet at the dealership."

"Now there's something you have in common with Brenna," Luke threw out. "No doubt you're both supporting Frank Hargrove and his agency for the terminally overinsured." He tossed the oily rag on the welcome mat. "I'm going to get cleaned up."

Clinton started to say something and then apparently thought better of it. "I'll see you later, Brenna," he said in a composed voice, walking to the door and looking neither left nor right. But Luke had already disappeared toward the downstairs bathroom without a backward look.

Brenna closed her eyes as the porch door banged behind Clinton. For years now she'd had a long string of peaceful, serene, quiet Sunday mornings. And then Luke McShane had come back. Goodbye, peace, she thought mournfully.

He emerged from the bathroom half an hour later, and Brenna chastised herself for being petty when she couldn't help comparing Luke's thick black hair, still glistening with droplets of water, to Clinton's thinning, moussed strands. She forced her eyes down to Luke's face, disconcerted to find him watching her solemnly as he tucked a fresh blue work shirt into his jeans.

"Something sure smells good," he said hopefully, and Brenna fought down a smile. He'd always loved her baking and she'd grown accustomed to his longing peeks at the oven when something was in it. He'd always praised her to the skies whenever he was talking her out of a piece of fresh bread or a hot cookie or whatever.

"Cinnamon rolls," she said. "They should be done in fifteen minutes."

"Good! That gives you time to change clothes. We're going to visit Dad. And we can bring him some of those rolls. He was always crazy about anything you made," Luke added cajolingly when he caught sight of her expression.

"Luke, I made the rolls for Clinton," she said firmly. "He took me out to dinner last week and I wanted to repay him."

"He won't miss two rolls," Luke assured her. "Now come on and get dressed so we can go."

In the end she did what he wanted, because that was easier than arguing with him. He was always too stubborn for his own good, she decided as she drizzled icing over the warm rolls. Then she made a last-minute check of her appearance in the mirror on the dining room wall. Not bad, she thought with a little smile. She'd pulled her hair back into a knot at the nape of her neck and put on her white cotton skirt that buttoned down the front and a dark green short-sleeved cotton sweater.

Back in the kitchen, she slipped on her sandals and began wrapping two of the rolls in foil. Luke came in the back door and stood staring at her appreciatively. "You look great, Bren," he said softly.

Flustered, Brenna made a show of folding the aluminum foil.

"Just two?" he said, sounding disappointed.

"I doubt if the hospital nutritionist is going to be thrilled with a whole batch of cinnamon rolls in your dad's room."

"Yeah, well, why don't you bring them all just in case," he suggested, giving her a crooked grin when she looked at him.

"Don't think I can't see where this is headed, Luke McShane," she assured him as she wrapped the rest of the rolls. "But you're getting one roll from this batch for yourself and that's all. The rest go to your dad and Clinton."

"Yes, ma'am," he said humbly as he escorted her out the door, but he kept rubbing his nose to hide his grin.

"We have to stop for gas," Brenna told him as they got into her car. "I'm running on fumes."

"Naw," he assured her, tapping the gas gauge with his finger. "You've got plenty."

"That gauge is broken. It always registers half a tank."

"See?" he said, tapping it again. "It moves."

"Of course it moves! You're thumping it. But that doesn't mean there's any gas in the tank."

"There has to be gas in the tank or it wouldn't register anything," he reasoned calmly.

Brenna gave up and threw her hands in the air in a silent plea for the heavens to deliver her from the pestilence of Luke McShane's logic.

"Hey, how about one of those cinnamon rolls?" he hinted.

"One," she informed him, "is all you get. So savor it, McShane."

"Yes, ma'am," he said, trying to tame an errant grin. "Oh, Lordy," he murmured in exaggerated ecstasy as he took a bite of the roll she handed him. "Heaven, Brenna, absolute heaven. Did I ever tell you you're the best cook on the face of the earth?"

"Whenever you wanted something in particular," she said immediately.

"Well, I meant it," he said, and then he frowned. "What's this?" he demanded, spitting a piece of the roll out into his hand.

"It's a raisin," she told him patiently. "They are edible, you know."

"Aw, Brenna, why'd you go and ruin a wonderful roll with raisins?" he complained, pitching the offending piece of fruit onto the highway.

"Luke! That's littering."

"It's a raisin, for God's sake. That's not littering." He glanced at her and rolled his eyes. "Do you expect some policeman to come after us with his lights flashing because of a raisin?"

"Clinton likes them with raisins," Brenna informed him defensively.

Luke gritted his teeth at that and plucked out the rest of the raisins. He made a show of setting each one in the ashtray before he devoured the roll. "How about another one?" he said.

"Luke! There won't be any left for Clinton."

"Give the auto king the raisins," he suggested grimly. He reached for another roll and Brenna stared out the window.

"Clinton's been very nice to me, you know," she said at last. "His parents, too."

Luke was silent a moment. "I'm glad someone's been looking after you, Bren," he said finally, grudgingly. "I hated thinking of you alone with no one to open tight jar lids for you or change a flat tire or take out the trash on a cold night." There was a softness in his voice that tugged achingly at her heart.

"I have a wrench for the jar lids," she said flatly, trying not to respond to the tone of his voice. "I call the garage when I get a flat. And I always take the trash out in the morning.''

"So you've been all right, then?" he asked. She could feel his eyes on her.

No! her heart cried. Sometimes things have been so lousy I can hardly stand it. Like a cold lonely bed in the middle of January or a soft April rain and no one to share it with. Like going to the cemetery and crying all by myself. But she didn't say any of it to him. She just stared out the window and tried not to think.

When she didn't answer he said, "Me, either," so quietly that she almost didn't hear him.

"We really messed things up," he said after another silence. She could feel him stealing glances at her as she forced herself to focus on the trees and small houses gliding past the car window. "Aren't you going to say anything?" he said.

"What is there to say?" she said wearily, finally turning and looking at him. He was frowning, and he immediately looked back out the windshield, avoiding her eyes.

"We could talk for once, Brenna, instead of both of us going off into our own little worlds."

"That was your trick, Luke, not mine." She saw his hands tighten on the steering wheel.

"Can't we stop blaming each other for once and just talk?" His voice was rough with anger.

"I'm not blaming you for the divorce," she said, willing her voice to remain neutral. "I was the one who filed. It's over, and I don't see any point in talking about it . . . about anything that happened."

"What happened to us, Brenna?" he asked sadly, sliding his eyes to hers, the sadness there making her look away. "When we were first married, we fought like cats and dogs, but we always worked everything out. Then, after . . . after what happened, it was like something turned to ice inside both of us. Like we'd never be warm enough to live again, let alone fight."

"What froze was your heart, Luke," she said quietly. "Mine, too. Sometimes it's the only way to survive the pain."

The high-pitched whine of the tires on the damp road seemed like a shriek in the car's sudden silence, and Brenna watched the telephone poles tick past like seconds on a clock. Luke was right. Something had frozen inside both of them after Dory died. And Brenna was afraid it was indeed their hearts.

"We did survive the pain, Brenna," he said at last, his voice threaded with a desolate timbre.

"Did we?" she asked wryly. "We couldn't face seeing each other, even as just friends, for almost ten years. We've both lived solitary lives since then, and if my guess about you is right, you've been as incapable of making any emotional commitments to anyone as I have." His flinch told her she was right. "I don't smile as easily as I used to, and I often wake up in the middle of the night for no reason at all." She took a ragged breath, emotion making her voice shake. "You tell me, Luke. Did we survive?"

Brenna's heart clenched when she saw James McShane lying against the white sheets of the hospital bed. He had always been a strong, vital man, like Luke, and she knew the enforced idleness of sickness was especially hard on him. He was as pale and thin as when she'd seen him last and she instinctively knew this was more than a simple case of the flu. She stole a quick glance at Luke and found him watching her carefully. He looked away and she sat down in the chair by the bed and clasped James's hand in her own, forcing herself to smile.

"The last time I saw you," she said gravely, "you were eating the blue-plate special I brought you from the café. Now tell the truth, James. It wasn't my cooking that put you in here, was it?"

A smile creased James's worn face and he chuckled. But his laughter quickly became a cough. "Brenna dear," he said when he got his breath back, "your chicken and dumplings rate as one of my fondest memories. But I can't say the same for Fergie's bran muffins. You've got to get him off that health-food kick."

"Is it bran with him now?" Luke said as he sat on the edge of the bed. "It used to be honey years ago. He claimed cane sugar was poison. I drew the line when he wanted me to put honey in my coffee."

Brenna went on chatting about the restaurant, her eyes coming to rest on Luke's strong fingers as they gently touched his father's frail arm. She'd forgotten how tender Luke could be, and she swallowed convulsively.

"Hey, Dad," Luke said softly when Brenna had fallen silent. "Look what Brenna made for you." He held up the aluminum-foil package of cinnamon rolls and grinned. Then he clucked and shook his head. "Unfortunately they're full of *raisins*."

"That's all right, son," James said with a smile. "I think I can overlook that. Brenna always brings me these when she comes to visit me at home."

"Yeah?" Luke said, looking at Brenna and studying her quietly. "So how come you never offered me any of those rolls when I came to see you?"

James shook his head. "Son, I'm awfully fond of you, but you see, we're talking about Brenna's cinnamon rolls here."

Father and son went on with their banter, but Brenna was still dwelling on what Luke had said about visiting. So he had come back to see his father other times. And apparently he had been very careful to avoid her. Waldo was a small town and it took some doing not to run into the entire population sooner or later. She was saddened that Luke had wanted her so thoroughly out of his life, out of his memory, that he would go to pains not to run into her. Dory's death had changed her and Luke both; it had certainly killed whatever feeling had existed between them.

It was obvious after fifteen minutes that James was tired out. Luke squeezed his hand and stood. "Listen, Dad, we'd better get going. I've got to get some work done on Brenna's car."

"You take care of her now, son," James called after them as they walked to the door. "That girl was the best daughter-in-law I ever had. I miss her."

Brenna turned back and tried to smile, but the effort was painful. She could see undisguised hope on James's face. He wanted her and Luke back together, and that was one thing she couldn't give him.

Brenna almost ran into a nurse as she left the room. The young woman gave her a warm smile. "Sorry. I didn't know James had company." Then her eyes slid to Luke. "Oh, Luke. Hi. I was just bringing your dad his medication."

Brenna didn't miss the light that came into the nurse's eyes when she saw Luke. He'd always had that effect on women, making them smile a little more broadly for him than for another man, their eyes following him almost automatically. But he seemed oblivious to this allure of his and he went on with his life, not thinking about the women in whose thoughts he lingered.

"How is he?" he asked the nurse in a low tone.

She gave him a sympathetic shrug. "He was awfully tired today."

Luke sighed and ran a hand through his hair. "Yeah, I know. Well, thanks, Julie."

"Sure."

Luke didn't speak all the way to the car. When they pulled out of the lot, he headed away from town. The expression in his eyes was muted, as though some invisible curtain had been drawn.

Brenna idly picked at one of the cinnamon rolls, her appetite gone but her hands in need of something to occupy them. Finally she had to ask the question that had been weighing on her mind. "What's wrong with James, Luke?"

"They still have to run some more tests, Brenna." He wouldn't look at her and his voice was tense.

Talk to me! she wanted to shout at him. For God's sake, trust me to share this with you. But she bit her lip instead and stared out the window. Their time for sharing was long past.

"Where are we going?" she asked instead.

"I just felt like driving. Like getting away for a while."

"Like running away," she said, chancing a look at him. His eyes probed hers briefly and then the curtain was drawn again and he stared ahead grimly. Brenna sighed. "Don't you remember? This is how it always was. When something went wrong you'd head for the race track. Job problems? Fight with the wife? Just get Luke McShane behind the wheel of a Turbo Z or whatever thing you drove, and after a few laps around the old track everything was fine."

"You could have come with me," he said quietly, and this time when his eyes met hers she saw emotion there—regret.

"I had a café to run," she said quickly.

His eyes held hers an instant longer before he looked back at the road. "The café and the race track served pretty much the same purpose, didn't they?" he said softly. "You did a lot of running away yourself."

She didn't have an answer to that because she realized he was probably right. She'd never thought of it like that before, but the café had increasingly become her refuge from the things she didn't want to face. In the days after Dory's death, when she and Luke were virtual strangers, she had gone to the café earlier than she had to and stayed later. She would come home exhausted. Then she was numb at least for a few hours, and she could sleep.

The car engine suddenly gave a few sputtering coughs. Brenna frowned. She looked at Luke and saw him pumping the gas pedal; a strange, disconcerted look was on his face. Luke was so seldom ill at east that Brenna guessed immediately what had gone wrong.

"We're out of gas, aren't we?" she asked dryly.

"No, Brenna, we're not out of gas," he said with certitude. The engine coughed again and the car lurched. "I'm pretty sure we're not out of gas," he said, his certitude diminished by two degrees or so.

"I knew it," Brenna said irritably. "You waltz around my car, you assure me—and you did *assure* me, Luke McShane—that I have plenty of gas, and then we end up stranded somewhere between Waldo and Chicago."

"Aw, Brenna, I'm sure there's enough gas to get us back to the house," he said with a renewed show of confidence.

"Right," Brenna said sweetly as the engine died. Staring straight ahead, silent, Luke guided the coasting car to the dirt shoulder.

Brenna looked around, wondering for the first time just where they were. Luke had taken a secondary road, so Waldo's traffic was nonexistent here. All around were trees and fields, and she couldn't quite get her bearings with no houses as landmarks.

"Where are we?" she demanded angrily as she jumped out of the car and slammed the door.

"About a mile out of town," Luke informed her with infuriating calm as he got out and came up behind her. "That's assuming your odometer works better than your gas gauge," he added dryly.

"I *told* you the tank was empty!" She began walking in the direction of town, trying to remember if the gas station that doubled as a quick shop would be closer than the two-pump independent station that overcharged.

"Look, Brenna, there's no point in getting upset," he said, walking sideways next to her so he could see her face.

She glanced at him and got even angrier when she saw that he had brought two more of the cinnamon rolls and was eating one. "Want a bite?" he offered, holding it out.

"No! I want a gas station!"

"Sorry, honey. Listen, why don't you wait here and I'll go find something." He was having to scurry faster as she increased her pace. "Okay, you don't want to wait here. Why don't you at least slow down and take it easy. You know how your hay fever kicks up when you're outside very long.''

Brenna stopped abruptly and turned to glare at him. ''Don't you get it, Luke? I don't want you going ahead to find a gas station! I don't want a bite of your cinnamon roll! And I don't want you worrying about my hay fever! I don't want anything from you!''

He watched as she gathered her dignity and trooped on ahead. She was right, he thought in resignation. He had no right to offer her anything. And yet he couldn't help himself. He wanted to do something for her, *anything*, if only she'd let him.

He shouldn't have asked her to come with him to see his father. He had known he'd come out of the hospital room in a hellish mood, but he should have thought of Brenna, of how she'd feel seeing James looking so sick and helpless. He clenched his hands into fists. Damn! Couldn't he do anything right? Now he'd gone and stranded them out here on some country road, and Brenna would start sneezing any minute now. He'd come back with hopes of . . . of what? Of finally telling her how sorry he was? Whatever he'd planned, he'd managed to foul it up royally.

Gritting his teeth, he caught up with her and fell into step.

Five minutes later she sneezed and Luke silently handed her his handkerchief. She took it without comment and wiped her nose.

''I had shots this spring,'' she said morosely. ''I don't know why I've still got hay fever.''

At least she wasn't furious with him any longer, he thought. That was one of the special things he remembered about her. Her temper could explode on a second's notice, but the anger dissipated as quickly. In their few short months together, they had fought and made up hundreds of times. It was as though they had battled to understand each other and build a bond together, but in the end that bond had crumbled.

He wished there wasn't such a sadness in her eyes. Beneath her feisty spirit, there was something else, something that hadn't been there when they married. It was like a bruise that wouldn't go away. You see it and think, That must have hurt terribly when it happened. And he could see it in Brenna now. But worse, he blamed himself for putting it there.

She sneezed again and blew her nose in his handkerchief. Luke closed his eyes tightly for a moment against the hot sun and the oppressive humidity. Swallowing the last of the sweet roll, he crumpled the foil and stuffed it into his pocket.

Luke opened his eyes the second Brenna made the sound. It was a low moan, and he thought she was in pain. She was standing stock still in the road, staring to the left. His eyes followed hers, and he blanched. A feeling of helplessness washed over him, the same feeling he'd had in Iowa when his car had spun out of control and headed for the wall.

"Oh, Lord," Brenna said, her voice catching. "We're behind the cemetery."

She started walking toward the low stone wall, and Luke wanted to catch her and pull her back, but he knew he couldn't stop her. So he did what he knew he had to do—he followed her.

They stepped over the wall and silently made their way across the lush, short grass, still wet with rain. Insects bit their legs and they slapped at them without conviction. The back of the cemetery was the oldest part. Slim, weathered and chipped gravestones sat at erratic angles. Some were so sunken that the name had nearly slipped underground to join the remains. *Edward Emerson, Feb. 19, 1841-April 24, 1887.* Luke wondered what the man had done in those forty-six years he was on earth. He had had a life. And Luke's baby had had none.

He hadn't been here in five years at least, but he could have found the grave unerringly, even without Brenna leading the way.

It was close to the front of the cemetery, under a huge elm tree not unlike the one under which he and Brenna had conceived Dory. His leg began to throb as they walked, but he took little notice. His world narrowed to the tiny tombstone they finally reached. A few sprigs of grass poked up in disarray around it. A vase of daisies sat in front, and their delicate petals made his heart clench. Brenna stood still, her head lowered as she lost herself in her own thoughts. She suddenly looked as fragile as glass.

"Why doesn't it get right again?" she wondered out loud, and he knew what she meant. *Her world.* Why hadn't her world ever righted itself? It hadn't righted itself for either of them.

"You think you'll forget it all one day," he said softly. "Like the incredible tininess of her fingers and toes, those little fingernails like slivers of shell. But it doesn't go away. When I'm eighty I think I'll still see her hands when I close my eyes."

"It doesn't hurt so much as it used to," Brenna said, her voice an aching sigh.

He looked at Brenna, at the curve of her cheek, like a peach with the first blush of ripeness, and he remembered so clearly how she had looked at the hospital, her skin pale and drawn, her eyes dark with grief.

They were to see their baby one last time before the doctors gave her to the undertakers—a horrible thought—and he had walked to Brenna's room as if he were a condemned man taking that final walk to the execution chamber.

The door was closed and he had pushed it open slightly. Brenna was sitting in the chair by the window, their baby in her arms, their lifeless baby whose fingernails were as delicate as slivers of shell. The light bathed the baby's sparse blond hair, the same light that touched Brenna's cheek and the tears that lay there.

He found he couldn't go in. He didn't know what to say. All he could do was stand there and watch his wife, while tears ran down his own face.

And now he felt just as helpless.

"I wonder what happened to those woodworking tools Dad gave me," he said to himself. Brenna looked at him through a sheen of tears.

She knew he was thinking of the crib his father and he had made for the baby, the crib that was in the garage along with the broken shovels and the old bags of fertilizer. He was standing only two feet from her, and yet they were in separate worlds, she thought with a pang. They were still powerless to comfort each other. Maybe if they had had another baby while they were still so young, if they had stuck it out together, things would be different now. They wouldn't be two strangers grieving over something that had happened ten years ago.

Almost without thinking, she reached out slowly and let her fingers brush his. She was surprised at the coolness of his hand. His fingers curled around hers, holding them against his rough palm, and Brenna finally found some relief from the horrible emptiness that assailed her.

They didn't look at each other, but a morning breeze stirred the grass and touched their faces and their hands where they were joined.

A car on the main road slowed, its tires splashing through puddles. Brenna didn't look; she wanted to stay like this for a while longer.

The car stopped and a door slammed. "Brenna!" came Clinton's voice. "I was worried about you. What's your car doing out on the county road?"

"We're out of gas," she said quietly. Luke dropped her hand, and Brenna felt the spell holding them in place crack and disintegrate.

"Well, what the hell were you doing out there anyway?" Clinton demanded. "I was out delivering that new antenna old Mr. Peterson ordered and I just happened to pass your car. I've been driving all over looking for you. I finally came down the main road and saw you here."

He hadn't acknowledged Luke's presence yet, and from the corner of her eye Brenna could see Luke standing impassively.

When he spoke, his voice was flat and without emotion. "Why don't you drive Brenna back home, Burgess?" he said. "I'll take care of Brenna's car."

Clinton glanced at Luke, then Brenna.

"You could ride back with us," Brenna said, not quite meeting Luke's eyes.

He shook his head. "I want to be alone for a while. I'll see you later."

So that was that, she thought. They'd stood together at their child's grave and still they hadn't come any nearer to reaching each other. They were both still alone.

"All right," she said wearily. "Come on, Clinton."

She glanced over her shoulder as she got in Clinton's car, and she saw Luke squat down by the grave and begin pulling up dandelions. He worked slowly and carefully and he didn't watch her leave.

Three

———

"Listen," Clinton said as he pulled into the dingy parking lot of the Sweet Treat Donut Shop. "I haven't had a thing to eat all morning. How about a cup of tea? You look like you could use one." He gave her an engaging smile and Brenna sighed. Clinton was apparently going to exercise his charm on her now.

"All right, Clinton. Just one cup. And I want coffee, not tea."

"Aw, come on, honey," he said as he helped her out of the car. He ruffled her hair and plopped his bulky arm around her shoulders. "You know you get all jumpy when you drink coffee. Herbal tea's much better for you." He nudged her arm and pointed to a dilapidated pickup truck beside the building. "Now there's someone who needs a new mode of transportation. I wonder if I ought to offer him three hundred down on a new car."

"Clinton, I'm old enough to decide what I want to drink," Brenna snapped as he opened the door, drawing his attention back to her. The arm abruptly dropped from her shoulders. Now she'd offended him, she thought as he stiffly escorted her to a small table and refused to meet her eyes. When she was seated, he went to the counter to order.

Brenna sighed. She'd once had an Irish Setter much like Clinton—overly sensitive, pushy and ingratiating to the point of nausea. His name was Harry, and he even resembled Clinton a bit around the eyes. His main goals in life were to eat on time, get out to chase a squirrel now and then and get someone to scratch his ears. That just about summed up Brenna's relationship with Clinton. He liked having her around to make him cinnamon rolls, to accompany him to business dinners and to sew buttons back on his cuffs. And if he could get her to scratch his back once in a while—right between the shoulder blades where he couldn't quite reach—then all the better. But that was as far as it went between them. They were old friends—maybe out of convenience—and they had long ago begun taking each other for granted.

"Now you eat this and you'll feel much better," Clinton advised, setting a cup of coffee and a large cherry turnover in front of her.

"Clinton, I appreciate your giving me a ride and getting me a cup of coffee, but I ought to get back. I'm worried about Luke having to walk."

"Now there's your problem," Clinton said around a big bite of donut. "You always worry about people you shouldn't give a second thought to. McShane's fine. Besides, it's his own fault he's stranded." Clinton turned to the elderly man sitting behind him on a stool at the counter and tapped him at the shoulder, effectively cutting off Brenna's irritated reply. "Hi, friend," he said enthusiastically. "Look, I couldn't help noticing your truck out there."

It took Clinton the better part of an hour to wrap up his deal with the hapless truck owner, and he crowed about his coup the entire drive to Brenna's house. She indulged him, realizing that Clinton Burgess, a man who clipped cartoons from *The New Yorker* and pretended to understand them, had to take his triumphs where he could find them. Brenna had once accused him of pining for the smog and traffic snarls of a big city, and he had mournfully concurred. He would have left Waldo long ago but for the weighty claim of his aging parents.

When he pulled into Brenna's lane, she saw Luke on the porch again, this time affixing the second shutter to the house. Her car was in front of the garage, a gas can beside it.

Brenna didn't miss Clinton's frown, and she found herself hoping Clinton would drop her off and leave. But luck wasn't with her.

Clinton got out of the car and slowly surveyed the situation while Luke continued hammering without missing a beat. "Your gutter's loose, you know that?" Clinton mused as Brenna came up beside him.

"Don't worry about the gutter," she told him, but she knew from the knitting of his brow that he was, indeed, going to worry about it. What was worse, he intended to do something, as well. Brenna glanced at Luke, deciding he wasn't listening.

"Hey, McShane!" Clinton called, rolling up his shirt-sleeves as he strode purposefully toward the porch. "Got a screwdriver on you?"

Luke turned around and glanced at Brenna before taking the screwdriver from his back pocket and handing it to Clinton. Brenna read his expression and hoped Clinton didn't; it was amusement.

"This looks like it'll do the trick," Clinton observed, grasping the stepladder that lay against the porch railing.

Luke rubbed his jaw. "It's too short, Burgess. You need an extension ladder for the gutters." So Luke had been listening after all.

"I can reach it. No problem," Clinton insisted. Luke shrugged and went back to hammering.

Brenna chewed her lip as Clinton set the stepladder up in front of the porch. Men, she thought in aggravation. Luke and Clinton were acting like two roosters who'd rounded opposite corners of the chicken coop and just discovered each wasn't the lone lord of the barnyard. And that really irritated Brenna, because neither man had shown a flicker of interest in her as a female in the past ten years. There was no way she was going to play adoring hen to their cock-of-the-walk act now.

"Did you have far to walk for gas?" Brenna asked Luke while Clinton carefully climbed the ladder.

Luke stopped hammering long enough to throw a "Yeah" over his shoulder.

"I was going to call the garage when I got back here," she said loudly as the hammering resumed.

"I appreciate that," he said, the hammering halted just long enough for his reply, which had been finely edged with sarcasm.

Brenna sat down heavily on the top porch step, narrowing her eyes to stare out past the stepladder to the mailbox at the end of her drive. It was sitting crooked. She ought to ask Luke to get the shovel. Correction, she ought to get the shovel herself and fix it. One day back and already Luke McShane had her brain cells out of alignment. Already he had her thinking there was *a man around the house*.

From atop the stepladder came the sound of the screwdriver being scraped against the gutter. A curious bumblebee came over to inspect Brenna's skirt. She brushed absently at it and then raised her voice over the hammering. "Did you get the fuel filter you needed?"

There was a short beat of silence after the hammering stopped. "No, I did not," Luke said slowly. "I probably could have walked the extra two miles from the gas station to the auto-parts store *before* I walked back to the car with the gas, but it seemed a little out of my way."

Brenna gritted her teeth. She dearly wanted to remind him that *she* was the one who had warned him the car was out of gas, but she decided to be big about the whole incident. "I could—" she began just ahead of the renewed hammering. She raised her voice over the sound. "I could go get you one!"

"Don't go to any trouble for me," came the terse answer between two whacks of hammer against wood.

The hell with being big about the whole incident, Brenna decided, brain cells clanging back into alignment. "Now, look here, Luke McShane!" she blazed, standing up and turning to face his stony back.

She didn't get any further. She heard the screwdriver scrape across metal in the distance and then Clinton's startled yelp. She turned in time to see one of his burnished leather shoes desperately reaching for the rocking ladder just before the ladder tilted one degree too far and two hundred pounds of Clinton Burgess came crashing to the ground in a rain of aluminum gutters.

Brenna jumped up from her perch, but Luke was already leaping from the porch, bypassing the steps altogether. Clinton was sitting on the ground, looking dazed and more than a little embarrassed, but he didn't appear to be hurt. Luke squatted beside him as Brenna removed the three-foot length of gutter lying across his ample middle.

"Do you think anything's broken?" Luke asked, inspecting Clinton.

"Shoot, yeah! The gutter's all broken to hell," Clinton mourned, sighing deeply as he surveyed the pieces scattered across the expanse of green yard.

"I meant bones," Luke said dryly.

Clinton shook his head with as much dignity as he could muster, and Brenna pulled Luke's handkerchief from his hip pocket. While gently wiping the smudge of grease on Clinton's brow, she tried to ignore the long wisps of his hair that had been jolted loose from their moussed bonds and now rippled in the breeze.

"Ow," he groaned as her hand brushed his nose. "I think I bumped my nose with my hand when I fell." And, indeed, his nose, now bright red, was beginning to swell at the end.

"Poor nose," Brenna murmured, having learned over the years of her friendship with Clinton that copious amounts of sympathy were required to soothe the injured male ego. "Come inside and I'll put some ice on it."

"Maybe you can put a sling on it, too," Luke suggested almost under his breath. Brenna darted him a quelling look.

They all turned at the sudden sound of a car door slamming, and Brenna saw her father and her Aunt Loraine hurrying from a vintage 1956 automobile. In the excitement of Clinton's fall, none of them had heard the car pull up. It must be some momentous occasion, Brenna thought distractedly, for Robert Hammond to take his beloved classic out of the garage long enough to risk getting a speck of dusk or—horror of horrors—a bird dropping on it.

"What are you doing, Clinton?" Robert asked, coming to a halt beside the pile of human beings and gutters on the ground and looking down curiously. "You all playing pickup sticks with the gutters?"

"Merciful heavens!" Loraine exclaimed, joining them. "If this isn't a mess!" She reached up to repin a stray wisp of gray hair into the everpresent bun at her neck, her fingers as brisk and efficient as they were at the café.

"I was putting the gutters up for Brenna," Clinton said, slightly altering the truth of the matter, "and the ladder went out from under me." He began pushing himself to his feet and Luke extended a hand, helping him up. Brenna hovered, still clutching Luke's handkerchief.

"Hired some handymen, did you, child?" Brenna's father teased her. Robert's eyes swung to Luke, then, and a boyish grin lit his face. At fifty-nine he still carried himself like someone much younger. Tall and thin, he was looselimbed and had a jaunty walk that had caught more than one widow's eye in Waldo. His gray hair was cut close, his grooming befitting the manager of the biggest discount store in Waldo.

"So, Luke, you're back." The two shook hands and then stood back to grin at each other. Luke and Brenna's father had always gotten along well, and Brenna had always suspected that Luke dropped in on her father on occasion after the divorce, much as she dropped in on Luke's father, but she couldn't prove it. Robert Hammond could be very close-mouthed when it suited him.

Clinton was gingerly feeling his nose, but no one seemed to notice.

"Listen, do you know I found the right set of hubcaps in a junkyard about twenty miles from here?" Robert asked eagerly. "A full set! Hardly dented either. And a decent shift knob. You know how long I've been without one." He nodded discreetly over his shoulder toward the car as though discussing a wife's errant cooking habits.

"Did you find any chrome knobs too?" Luke asked, obviously interested.

"You bet he did," Loraine threw in. "Took 'em right down to Custom Rebuilding where you used to work and had Avery install them."

"Yeah?" Luke said, his grin broadening. "Hey, how is Avery anyway? I've been meaning to drive by and show him what I did with my car."

Robert's eyes glowed with the fervor of fireworks in a night sky. "Son, I'd sure like to go along when you do. Been itching to see the guts of that car after it's modified."

"Well, heck, let's do it now," Luke said amiably. He reached out for his handkerchief without looking at Brenna and his fingers brushed hers tantalizingly, reminding her of the feel of his hand at the cemetery. Without thinking, she tightened her fingers on his, her knees weakening in response to his touch as though she'd climbed up and down that stepladder a few hundred times.

There was an almost imperceptible returning pressure from Luke's fingers, and then they were gone, taking the handkerchief with them. Brenna swore at herself mentally. Why don't you just announce in the *Waldo Gazette* that the man is getting to you? she chastised herself angrily. Her heart was still pounding from his touch, even as he blithely strode off toward his car with Robert and Loraine, leaving Brenna in a rising state of indignation and disappointment that he hadn't invited her along. Luke seemed to take for granted that she'd rather stay here and rub liniment on Clinton's wounded nose than ride with him to the body shop where he used to restore cars when he wasn't racing.

As if reading her thoughts, Clinton cleared his throat. "Is the ice in the freezer?" he asked, overdoing the male helplessness a bit, in Brenna's estimation.

"No, Clinton, I keep it in the microwave," she said deadpan, her eyes still on Luke's retreating figure, that devil-may-care thrust of his hips making her heart attack her ribs again.

When she looked back at Clinton and met his puzzled eyes, she sighed and let go of some of her anger toward Luke. Clinton couldn't help it if he was dense about her dry jokes or if he treated his own minor injuries like major operations or...*or if he wasn't Luke,* her pounding heart added.

"Come on," she said. "I'll fix an ice pack for you." Resolutely, Brenna started up the porch steps, Clinton in tow. She turned when she heard an engine gunning and watched with helpless resignation as Luke's car sped down her drive, the three people in it laughing companionably. Damn. What bothered her most was that she could feel the salt burn of one or two unwelcome tears pricking her eyes. She had to admit to herself that Luke still had the power to make her that unhappy. She swore to herself again and then marched into the house.

Clinton apparently didn't read her expression well enough to know he ought to keep quiet. "You shouldn't be letting him stay here, Brenna," he began. "You know he— Mmphhh! Take it easy with that ice pack!" He shot her a reproachful glance and resettled the ice pack on his nose. "Now, as I was saying, Brenna—"

"Don't push it, Clinton," she warned him, occupying her hands with straightening up the kitchen.

"*I'm* the one who had to deal with your broken heart the last time," he went on. "And I'm sure you expect me to pick up the pieces this time, too."

Brenna rounded on him carefully, the deliberate slowness of her words a clear indication of the emotion behind them. "Clinton, I told you before that I appreciated you and your folks taking me to their cabin after... after the baby died. But I've thought about it these last years, and I think I was wrong to have gone then. Luke and I killed whatever chance we had of making our marriage work when both of us ran off in separate directions. I have to take some of the blame for that, and I'm not proud of it."

Clinton snorted through the ice pack. "Oh, hell, Brenna! You can't see the forest for the trees. You were well rid of the man. He was never any good for you. I told you that when you married him."

"I remember, Clinton," she said coolly. "All my life you've told me what was good for me and what wasn't. You would have made an excellent mother hen."

"You'd better listen to me this time, Brenna," he warned her. "You're making a big mistake even letting that lowlife put one foot on your porch. He's no good now and he never was."

"That's enough, Clinton," she said with deadly calm. "I think it's time you left."

He sat up straight in surprise, assessing her sincerity. Apparently realizing she was serious, Clinton stood up with as much dignity as he could muster with an ice pack resting on his nose and walked to the door. He paused before pushing open the screen and salved his wounded pride with one last parting shot. "You're the same as me, Brenna. We don't open up to others easily, and we don't take to change too well. I used to want to live in the city, but now I'm happy here. There's no point in wanting things you aren't suited for. I think you'll come to realize in time that I'm right."

He walked through the door, then shut it quietly. His car started a few moments later and Brenna watched it make its slow, ponderous way down the drive. She couldn't help thinking what Luke would have done had the fight been with him. He would have had his say no matter how angry she was and then he would have slammed the door off its hinges on his way out.

But then, maybe Clinton was right, she thought sadly. She was too orderly and controlled to be suited to a man who could make a scene like that.

The truth of the matter was, she hadn't been all that sure who she was since Luke came back. Maybe she hadn't been sure before he came, either, but at least she'd been, well, content. She had her life, and she had come to terms with it. The problem was that after one look at Luke McShane, the terms of her life looked more like terms of surrender than victory. And when Luke had kissed her, she'd had a gnawing urge to tear up the peace treaty she'd negotiated with her life. Luke had an uncanny ability to make her want more, to make her feel half alive without him around. And right now she could throttle him for making her feel that way.

She started walking, her favorite tension-defusing activity, and she absently brushed the brownish leaves of the apple trees as she strode purposefully past them, reminding herself to spray them for whatever fungus they had.

She kicked at dirt clods and vigorously ground down the sifted mounds of earth pushed up by moles. A former owner had used the land adjoining the apple trees as pasture, and a sagging wire fence marked its perimeters. Cedar trees, once confined to a small clump in one corner, now crept outward, even daring to crop up like sturdy foot soldiers right against the fence. Their compact branches prickled her face and arms as she climbed over the fence.

The walk wasn't relaxing her at all. Instead, she seemed to gather speed and frustrated energy as she pushed doggedly through the pasture, mashing down orchard grass and foxtail. Her skirt caught on a wild rose bush and she savagely pulled it loose, swearing tightly when a thread came with it. She finally came to a stop beside the pond and sank to the ground, her chest heaving with labored breathing. She sneezed once and cursed her stupidity at not bringing a tissue.

What was the matter with her? she demanded of herself in exasperation. She had never before stormed out of the house to stalk the brush and bramble of her farm in a skirt. She was always too fastidious for that. The skirt should have been hanging in a closet, and Brenna should have been wearing sensible jeans. But she wasn't, and unreasonably she blamed Luke. She hadn't known up from down since he arrived on her doorstep the day before.

It was just a matter of making an adjustment, she told herself. She just had to get used to him being around again, and then when he left things would return to normal.

When he left... That was the devil that was snagging her the way the rose thorn had snagged her skirt. She always had to deal with that when it came to Luke. It stood between them like that fence post dividing the pasture. His leaving was inevitable. And Brenna with her staid, predictable life couldn't handle that coming and going habit of his even though she no longer loved him. Even if the coming occurred only every ten years or so.

His taking her father and aunt to see Avery had reawakened that aching feeling of being left out, of not being able to run fast enough to keep up with Luke McShane. And she didn't want to be reminded of that.

Angrily, she aimed a small stone at a branch half submerged on the opposite side of the pond, and missed by a mile. But the sound of the stone hitting the water was loud and resonant.

As was the sound of the voice behind her.

"Lousy aim, Brenna. I bet you haven't thrown a stone in ten years."

He was right, she acknowledged as she composed her face before looking over her shoulder. He had had her throwing things all the time when they were married—stones into ponds, softballs into his mitt and occasionally a potholder at his aggravating, teasing mouth when he pushed her just an inch too far with his bawdy good humor.

Luke knew why she didn't turn around right away. He remembered that much from their short time together. Brenna was always watchful, careful to hide her emotions from him. And he blamed himself for most of that. Hell, when she had wanted to talk, he had always been on his way out the door to some race.

He made himself smile. "You're going to feel like throwing more stones when I tell you what's waiting at the house."

She eyed him warily. "Did you tow another wreck back?"

He shook his head. "Your brother Joe dropped by. He wants to know why you didn't inform him I was here. He sounded pretty put out about it."

"Oh, great," she said dispiritedly. "Now we can have a family reunion and everyone can demand to know why I didn't send out announcements about your arrival."

He started to sit down beside her, but she stood up abruptly, so he remained standing.

The drought had taken its toll on the pond, he thought as he glanced over her shoulder. The level was down and the water was a brackish brown.

He remembered his plans to stock the pond with bass and how he and Brenna had driven to Missouri to buy the fingerlings. They'd fought all the way because Brenna, for some insane reason, insisted they should be getting trout instead of bass. He'd tried to explain that trout needed flowing water, that they wouldn't survive in a pond. "But bass are so ugly with those big mouths," she protested.

"Honey, we're going to eat the fish, not enter them in a beauty contest," he'd countered. Brenna had opened her mouth to reply, and then apparently the whole thing struck her as funny and she began laughing. His own chuckle grew until he had to pull the car to the shoulder, and their laughter echoed against the weathered limestone rock cuts bordering the road. He'd kissed her then, he remembered, and the taste of her came back to him as clearly as if it had been yesterday.

"What happened to those fingerlings we put in the pond?" he asked, and he saw the ghost of a smile touch her mouth before she sobered again.

"I guess we lost them," she said quietly. "I never saw any fish in the pond after that."

He nodded silently, thinking of all the other things they'd lost. They'd paid a heavy price for loving each other, and eventually that price drove them apart. His gaze moved to her hair and he saw the way the trembling breeze touched it, died down, then returned to touch it again. The sun did the same with her face. It hid behind a cloud and then slid out to stroke buttery light across her nose and the smattering of freckles there. His gaze dropped to her lips and his mouth went dry. Seeing Brenna again had been more painful than he'd ever thought it would be, and part of that was the unanswered hunger that gnawed his stomach every time he was around her.

He wasn't going to touch her. Hell, he had all kinds of good intentions when she was out of sight. But let her get within reach and his hands seemed drawn to her like metal filings to a magnet.

He didn't even recognize the moment his wants became reality, the moment when his hand was no longer hooked in the waistband of his jeans but was touching her shoulder, his thumb drawn to the smooth plane of her collar bone. He saw her stiffen slightly, saw her eyes narrow in wariness, but he was powerless to stop his hands from gently pulling her to him.

One taste, his mouth promised. One taste and this hunger will be gone.

But Luke's hunger was a strange beast. His lips brushed hers, and he felt a thin tremor run through her. It made him want to hold her tightly to him, to banish the ghosts that stood between them and made this simple kiss so impossible. His mouth gentled and began a tender assault on hers. He felt her resistance, and he ached for the pain he knew was inside her. Then he felt the resistance ebb ever so faintly until her mouth molded itself to his. Her palms came to rest against his chest.

The hunger grew. He wanted more than a kiss, but he knew he was stealing even this much from her. He was hurting her without meaning to and without being able to stop. And yet time stood still when they came together like this.

His mouth moved over hers restlessly, and still the hunger gnawed him with relentless sharpness. *I always wanted more of you, Brenna, more than you ever knew.* Even the speed and exhilaration he craved at the track couldn't wipe out all the need. There was always one corner of him aching for Brenna.

He cursed that corner when he lifted his mouth from hers and saw the bruised, hurt look in her eyes. Her hands fell away from him as though burned. He realized in that moment just how hard she was fighting this attraction that had always existed between them.

"Brenna, I didn't—" he began with a gravelly hoarseness in his voice, but she cut him off, taking two steps back, her eyes blazing with anger and pride.

"The fingerlings are gone, Luke," she said, her voice level. There might have been a sheen of moisture in her eyes, or it might have been the sunlight. "And I expect you will be, too, soon enough. Don't make it any harder for me."

When she rounded the house, she could see her father and Loraine sitting on the top step of the porch, sipping iced tea and looking completely at ease. Brenna stopped a second to still her throbbing pulse. Damn Luke! Damn him for coming back here and for making her feel like this again. A tender look from him, a gentle touch, the texture of his mouth on hers, and she felt her blood pound like a filly turned into the pasture after a long winter in the barn. When Luke's lips had taken hers by the pond, old feelings had flooded back, unbidden and unwanted, and suddenly the sky was bluer, the flowers sweeter, the wind more caressing than they had ever been before. A woman could grow to like those feelings a little too much, could come to look forward to a certain man's touch, then when he was gone she would go through a private hell all over again.

She glanced over her shoulder and saw that he was still far behind her and was making no attempt to catch up. He was limping slightly again, she noticed. Weariness seemed to do that to him. Forcing herself to take a deep breath, she stepped to the front of the house.

Joe jumped up from the bottom step as soon as he saw her and demanded, "What's Luke doing here?"

"Hello to you, too, Joe," she said dryly. "So nice to have you drop by for a visit."

Her older brother, a taller version of Brenna, with the same red-gold hair, though his tended more to red, had the grace to look slightly abashed before he resumed his interrogation. "Well, shoot, Brenna, I figured you'd go off the deep end and slam the door in his face if he ever showed up here."

"Now, son," their father drawled, shaking his head. "I'm beginning to think I ought to demand my money back from that college that gave you a diploma. That's not a real smart way to phrase things."

"For crying out loud!" Joe said in exasperation. "Since when has tact worked with Brenna?"

Robert clucked and Loraine rolled her eyes.

"For your information, Joe," Brenna said coolly, "Luke's dad is in the hospital and Luke's staying here to be close to him."

Joe made a noncommittal sound and Brenna crossed her arms. She didn't owe explanations to anyone, least of all her family, all of whom tended to become overly involved in her life.

"Well, this is a fine time to show up," Joe muttered, digging his toe in the soft ground and talking more to himself than to Brenna. "If he was going to come back, I'd have thought it'd be after he damn near killed himself in that crackup."

"What crackup?" Brenna demanded sharply.

Joe looked up, taking a long appraising look at her. He shrugged. "It was just an accident."

"He crashed in a race?" she pressed. Joe looked over her shoulder uncomfortably.

"As you can see, I found her," Luke said from behind her. When Brenna anxiously turned around to ask him how bad the accident was, she found him studying her gravely.

"Luke, you didn't tell me—" she began, but he interrupted her smoothly.

"Look at you, Brenna," he clucked, making a mock survey of her state of dishevelment. "You've torn your skirt and there's dirt on your face, *and* your nose is running. Now how am I going to take you to the Knights of Columbus barbecue tonight like that?"

"The Knights of Columbus barbecue?" she repeated vaguely, dabbing at her nose with the handkerchief he handed her.

"The barbecue I always looked forward to all year," he informed her patiently. "Chicken and spareribs and probably a good band to boot."

"Your leg," she said, frowning and trying to get back to the subject at hand. "Did you hurt it in—"

"Honestly, Brenna," he said, raising his shoulders in a parody of exasperation. "Follow the conversation, honey. I'm asking you to the barbecue." And I don't want to talk about the accident, his dark eyes plainly said when she looked into them.

She supposed she'd forfeited the right to worry about him anymore. They were no longer married, and he didn't have to answer her questions about his injuries. Clearly, he didn't want to, either.

"Don't humor me, Luke McShane," she warned him, deciding to let her questions go for now. "You know I love a barbecue even more than you do."

His blue eyes crinkled when he smiled, leaving her mesmerized. "Then put on your dancing shoes tonight," he murmured, his mouth crooked slightly, reminding her of aeons ago when they had danced at the barbecue as husband and wife, when there had been no need to fight errant feelings of desire.

But Brenna had to fight those feelings now. If she looked into his eyes a moment longer she was afraid she would groan under the aching weight of memories.

But it was Luke who looked away first—regretfully, she imagined—and turned to Brenna's brother. "Come here a minute, Joe," he said, looping an arm around Joe's shoulders and walking him away from the house. "There's a little matter I wanted to talk to you about."

Brenna started to follow them, a question rising to her lips. Since when did they think they could keep secrets from her? But Robert called to his daughter. "Brenna, honey, do you think you could press the wrinkles out of my golf shirt for the barbecue? I had it folded in my drawer all winter."

"Your bright red golf shirt?" Brenna asked, narrowing her eyes at her father. He nodded. "The one that Bishop Barbara said makes you look like Arnold Palmer?"

"Now, honey, don't call the woman that," her father protested.

"Dad, all of Waldo calls Barbara the Bishop." Brenna heard Luke and Joe mention Denny, but despite straining her ears she couldn't decipher what they were saying. "And with good reason. She's been married so many times she's seen the inside of more churches than any bishop."

"And she doesn't stay married long enough to get the rice out of her hair," Loraine added, coughing discreetly when Robert shot her a leveling glance. "Well, if the shoe fits, dye it to match your clothes," Loraine murmured. In her entire life, Brenna had never heard her aunt get an old saying right.

"You plan to dance a little with the Bishop tonight, do you?" Brenna asked indulgently.

Her father suddenly occupied himself with an earnest study of his fingernails. "Might," Robert said succinctly.

"Well," Brenna said philosophically, "I guess you'd better bring your golf shirt over then so I can iron it. You don't need your black silk tie cleaned or anything, do you?"

"I'm not ready to have my 'marrying' tie pressed, thank you," he said dryly. Loraine chuckled. That famous black silk tie was the one he had worn when he married Brenna's mother, and as a joke Denny had worn it when he married his now ex-wife. Robert had grumbled after Denny's divorce that he knew the marriage was doomed when he found a cake stain on his tie after the wedding. Luke hadn't worn it when he married Brenna, and she had later thought that a bad omen.

"Did Clinton get his nose fixed up?" Loraine asked as Brenna started up the steps.

"No," Brenna said, darting a glance over her shoulder at Luke and Joe still bent in earnest conversation. "It's still out of joint."

Luke pronounced her pretty enough to ride in his bright red car, but Joe couldn't see the sense of it. "Luke, you're not taking that car to the barbecue?" he said in disgust. "Hell, all that mud out there and you'll have to park it under the pine trees. Oh, geez, that pine pitch is murder on cars."

Brenna rolled her eyes. "Don't take your car," she told Luke. "It might be the death of Joe."

"I'm not taking a pretty lady like you in that rattletrap of yours," Luke said firmly. "Now get in."

He kept eyeing her sideways during the drive, and finally he said, "I like that dress. Is it new?"

Brenna nodded. "Right out of the Penney's catalog." The dress was an off-the-shoulder cotton jersey in a bright pink print that made her look almost like a gypsy. She'd enhanced the comparison with big gold hoop earrings and kohl shadow around her eyes.

"Did you, uh, pick up your nightgown yet?" Luke asked, raising his eyebrows curiously.

"Not yet," Brenna said primly, hiding her grin when he looked disappointed.

"Maybe I could drop by and get it for you," Luke volunteered as he pulled the car onto the dirt road into the Knights of Columbus grounds and headed for the makeshift parking lot.

"That won't be necessary," Brenna informed him. When she saw the incipient question in his twinkling blue eyes she added, "And neither will the modeling of said nightgown."

"My spirit is crushed," Luke mourned, grinning nonetheless as he reached across her to open her door. Brenna caught a sudden whiff of a woodsy cologne mingled with the scent of freshly washed hair. He was gone the next instant, and Brenna sat stock still watching him round the car, his new jeans hugging lean, muscled hips and thighs. His lithe long-legged stride brought him to her side, and he held out his large, firm hand. Brenna thought fleetingly of the comfort in that hand at the cemetery, and then his fingers closed over her own.

The night air was damp and heavily perfumed with honeysuckle and pine. A breeze blew fitfully across the grounds, swinging the strings of yellow lights and wafting laughter from the booths where mostly men and children played darts and poker and a Ping-Pong ball game called I Dood It.

Luke kept hold of her hand as they made their way through the crowds around the various barbecue pits and game booths. He was wearing a black shirt with white stripes circling the chest and running down the inside of the three-quarter sleeves. He had left two metal snaps open at the neck and a sprinkling of dark hair showed through. He looked damn good, and she was pretty sure he knew it. There weren't many places in Waldo where a man could strut his stuff, so a barbecue was a real event.

A few men stopped throwing darts long enough to call to Luke. He called back and gave them a nod before moving on. Brenna wasn't unaware of the appreciative female glances following them, but Luke seemed oblivious.

They stopped at a beer stand and Luke got them two paper cups of what was on tap. Nearby the country-western band was warming up and testing amplifiers. She and Luke leaned against a tree, watching them.

When she glanced back at Luke, his eyes were on her and Brenna felt her skin flush with a heat that wouldn't be cooled by the breeze. She took a quick sip of her beer as the band's leader stepped up to the microphone. To enthusiastic applause he welcomed everyone to the barbecue and announced that the band would play until eleven.

Brenna lowered her cup and Luke smiled, a smile that under the shadows of the tree seemed to come from the boy she'd married so long ago. His hand touched her face, stealing her breath and her composure, but his finger was only brushing away the foam that was bursting in tiny bubbles on her upper lip. Brenna could feel a steady pounding in her ears, she wasn't sure if it was her heart or the electronically amplified bass on stage.

"Let's dance," Luke said. She read the words on his lips rather than heard them.

He took the beer from her immobile fingers and set it on a nearby picnic table. "Hi, Luke," came a low, inviting female voice from the table, but Luke only nodded and smiled, his eyes never leaving Brenna's.

There was no formal dance platform, only a cleared grassy area in front of the band. Luke led Brenna there, keeping them both in the tree shadows and away from the other couples dancing.

The band played mournful country songs filled with images of loss and pain. The music itself was slow and sad, and Brenna didn't resist when Luke pulled her even closer to him. Her hand crept up his back until her finger could stroke the nape of his neck where his dark hair curled tightly with abandon. A throat growl in her ear let her know he was enjoying this.

Brenna could feel his body molded against hers, hard and male and full of desire. He let go of her hand and draped both arms around her waist, dropping his head until his lips brushed her neck. "You smell good," he murmured.

It was only soap—she'd grown so unaccustomed to wearing perfume that she'd forgotten it—but still she felt the tingling satisfaction of receiving a man's compliment.

The band was tireless, and so was Luke. He danced each song with her, holding her close and making her body tremble with the need to be held even closer. She was letting herself have this one night with Luke, letting herself revel in the hard contours of his body against hers, because they were among people here and nothing would come of their closeness.

She saw her father dance by once, whirling the Bishop across the grass, his red shirt glowing in the yellow lightbulbs framing the stage. Luke was still swaying slowly in the shadows, seemingly oblivious to the peppery quickstep going on around them. Brenna leaned against Luke, breathing in his male scent along with the pine and the oily sweetness of funnel cakes frying somewhere close. "You're so pretty in that dress," Luke whispered, and she looked up into a shadowy smile and blue eyes like the ocean in moonlight.

His lips brushed her forehead, and they virtually stopped dancing. They just stood there under the tree swaying softly against each other. "Brenna," he said hoarsely. There was a new note in his voice, a ragged torment she hadn't heard before. His eyes glowed with a fire he was struggling to control. "It's like it used to be," he whispered. "I didn't think I'd feel it so much, being here with you."

She knew what he was feeling because she was feeling it, too. He wanted her the way a man wanted a woman, the way he'd wanted her so long ago.

"Luke, we're not the same two kids," she said sadly. "It couldn't ever be the same."

He was silent a moment, not moving at all now, and then he said, "Couldn't it?" There was such a sadness in his voice that she wanted to put her arms around him and hold him for all the times they should have held each other and didn't. She was teetering on the edge of falling into that abyss again, that abyss of loving Luke McShane and getting only pain in return.

She whispered his name and she saw him take a shaky breath. "Brenna, don't," he murmured. She realized that her whisper had been an invitation, even as her heart denied it. "I promise I won't ever hurt you again, Brenna," he said at length in a low voice. "Don't—"

The rest of his warning was lost as Clinton appeared beside them, a scowl creasing his face. "Surely I can have one dance with Brenna," he said to Luke with a dry sarcasm. Oh, Lord, Brenna thought frantically. She could smell beer hanging around Clinton, and she knew from experience that he was no drinker.

There was a charged moment when both men just stood there looking at each other, then Luke swung his gaze to Brenna. Whatever he had been fighting to control a moment before was gone and now only banked embers smoldered in his eyes. "I was going to leave anyway," he said. "I'll tell your dad to make sure you get home." And he was gone, disappearing into the trees leading to the parking area.

Clouds were rolling in and the breeze had turned chilly. The stars were twinkling out one by one as a deeper shade of night poured across the sky like spilled molasses creeping over a tabletop. The yellow lights jangled in the wind, and Brenna stifled the need to run after Luke. He hadn't even brought a jacket with him, and now he was headed heaven knew where. She had always hated the thought of him off by himself, cold and lonely.

She had seen the struggle within his eyes tonight and she had felt it inside herself. What were they fighting so hard? Each other or something they each harbored within?

Clinton's hand was tight on Brenna's arm as he maneuvered her toward the lights. She danced mechanically with him, growing colder by the moment. She looked up and suddenly realized that he had covered his nose with white adhesive tape. Someone bumped them as they danced and a male voice called out, "What happened, Clinton? Did you run into a door or a frisky female?"

"Did a little handiwork at Brenna's," Clinton called back, his voice a trifle unsteady from the beer. "Almost broke it."

The banter went on, but Brenna was listening for the sound of Luke's car starting up. A car left the grounds by the lower gate, kicking up gravel, but when Brenna looked over Clinton's shoulder she couldn't see it in the dark.

She was home by eleven. She brewed coffee and waited for the sound of his car. By midnight she had taken a quick bath and put on her warm terry robe as the wind began gusting. At two she still lay awake in bed, listening to the wind and waiting for the car that never turned into her drive.

Four

It was ten minutes after eight on Monday morning when Brenna snatched her purse from her car and ran through the door of the Chestnut Tree Cafe. She jangled the bell over the door with such force that it went on tinkling a good five seconds. Her Aunt Loraine looked pointedly at her watch.

"You must have had something mighty interesting to do at home last night after the barbecue," she observed as she carried four plates of scrambled eggs and a bottle of catsup to a table by the window.

Brenna took a quick glance around and saw the usual morning crowd—the local telephone company linemen; the three elderly Conley brothers who each owned a dairy farm and who had married sisters, none of whom could cook; Loretta Harpole from the Clip 'N Curl beauty shop; and Thaddeus and Cloris Hennesy, the local celebrities. The Hennesys were sitting with a couple Brenna didn't know and she assumed from the horse van outside that they were from out of town and on their way to the county fair.

Cloris and Thaddeus were well into the story of their claim to fame, and Cloris was pushing aside the red gingham curtain to point up the road. "It was right up there in Howard Starn's field. See? There's a big black spot there where it burned the ground. It was a big spaceship, wasn't it, Thad?"

Thaddeus pondered this. "Ain't real sure," he said at last. He took the toothpick out of his mouth and fixed the couple with a telling look. "You see, I was hypnotized to forget all about it."

The couple's mouths became round little o's, and Cloris nodded in satisfaction. "We was on board and everything. And let me tell you, the refrigerator they had on that thing would beat my old one any day." She raised her eyebrows and confided, "Thad and me, we figure it was for keeping specimens in. You know—people. At least that's what the man from the magazine thought when we told him."

So then Cloris went into the story of how the reporter had come to Waldo to interview her and Thaddeus after they wrote the editor with their story of the spaceship that landed in Waldo, Illinois, and hypnotized two residents.

Brenna rounded the counter and leaned over to murmur to Loraine, "That burned spot on the ground gets bigger every time they tell that story."

"Funny how they never mention that Howard Starn said he made that black spot burning trash there," Loraine added in a low voice, reaching up to readjust the pins in her hair. "What's that?" she asked, nodding toward the package in Brenna's hand.

Brenna looked down and realized she had grabbed the Penney's package along with her purse. Quickly she set it on the shelf behind the counter. "This? Oh, just something from Penney's."

"I can see the name on the bag," Loraine pointed out. "I was just wondering what it was."

Brenna cleared her throat. "I thought since I was so late anyway, I'd run by there and pick it up. They aren't usually open this early, but I went to high school with the clerk and I ran into her at the gas station this morning and she was on her way to work..." Brenna trailed off, realizing she was babbling. "Well, I guess I'd better go see if I can help Fergie." She pushed open the swinging door to the kitchen, fully aware that her aunt was still watching her and was even more curious now about what was in the bag.

She came back from the kitchen carrying a fresh batch of Fergie's bran muffins, with Fergie right on her heels. He was a little man with bright red hair liberally tinged with gray, and right now he was full of enthusiasm. "And if we put oat bran in the scrambled eggs it would up everybody's fiber intake," he was saying.

"Lord, Fergie," Brenna said impatiently. "None of our customers is going to stand still for that."

"Why, sure they would," he protested.

"You go ask them," Brenna suggested. "We'll see."

Loraine had edged closer to the bag on the shelf and was just about to open it when Brenna pulled it out of reach. "Will you leave that alone!" she said.

"What's that?" Fergie asked.

"Don't ask me," Loraine said, clearly offended. "It's something from Penney's, and Brenna's acting like it's a dang package from the governor himself."

"It is *not*—" Brenna began, but she stopped short as the bell over the door tinkled and in walked Luke McShane, looking tired and disheveled but still in possession of his jaunty walk. Brenna scanned him quickly for damage, and she let out her breath when she decided he looked none the worse for wear. He had never come back to the house last night, and now relief that he was all right gave way to irritation.

Luke came straight to the counter and sat down in front of them. "Good morning," he said gravely despite the smile hovering around his mouth.

"Good morning," Brenna said coolly, not daring to ask him where he'd been while she had this audience assembled around her. "Are you here for breakfast or have you already prevailed on someone else's hospitality for that?"

Both Fergie and Loraine shot Brenna looks that said they were appalled at her rudeness with Luke. "Brenna, the man *is* a customer," Loraine reminded her niece. Turning to Luke, she shook her head. "She's been all stirred up this morning, ever since she walked in here with some secret in a Penney's bag."

"Don't you have people who need coffee refills?" Brenna asked pointedly.

"What Penney's bag?" Fergie asked.

"And you," Brenna said to him, "had better check the kitchen. I'm not serving anyone burned pancakes this morning."

When she turned back to Luke, having dispersed her grumbling hangers-on, he was grinning. "Penney's bag, huh?"

"What is so interesting about a Penney's bag?" Brenna demanded in a voice that stilled conversation throughout the café and turned heads in her direction.

"Nothing," Luke said innocently, but his mouth was twitching. He pulled a coffee-stained menu from its holder between the salt and pepper and pretended to study it. "You don't have any cinnamon rolls this morning, do you?" he asked.

"Not this morning," she said, covertly studying his face. He looked tired and she worried that he hadn't slept. "Do you want some coffee? Unless you already had some, that is. Wherever you were."

Luke tried to hide his grin behind the menu, not entirely successfully. "Coffee would be fine, thanks, Brenna."

"Some pancakes?" she suggested. "Maybe some eggs. You look like you could use the protein."

"You sound like Fergie," he told her, letting the grin loose this time. "I don't want you worrying about me, Brenna."

"I don't worry about you," she insisted. "What you eat for breakfast is none of my concern. Or where you sleep for that matter," she added peevishly. The man was doing this deliberately, annoying her by keeping his whereabouts secret.

She turned to go to the kitchen, but Luke's hand closed around her wrist, taking her by surprise and making her stomach jump as though she'd just crested the first hill on a roller coaster and sat poised over empty space. She made the mistake of looking into his face and was suddenly pulled into deep blue eyes that had turned serious. "You *were* worried, weren't you?" he asked softly.

"Don't be ridiculous!" She stood stiffly, and then he began an unconscious massage of the sensitive underside of her wrist with his thumb, his eyes still probing hers. Zoom! Down went the roller coaster and Brenna's stomach with it.

"You *do* care a little, despite everything, don't you?" he insisted. When she remained silent he sighed wearily. "We're both too full of pride and silence, Brenna," he said gently. "I'll tell you where I spent last night."

"It makes no difference to me," she said in a voice far cooler than the temperature of her skin where his thumb stroked. "We're not married anymore. And when we were, I assure you I grew quite accustomed to going to bed alone. I didn't know then who shared your bed, and I don't care now."

"No other woman ever—" he began, his eyes blazing, and she immediately regretted having said that. She knew he had been faithful to her during their brief marriage. With her younger brother, Denny, trailing after Luke at every race, it would have been impossible for her not to know if he hadn't.

"Hey, Luke!" called out Jason Conley, who, at seventy-five, was the youngest of the three brother farmers. "That your car out front?"

Jason shambled over in his bib overalls and Luke slowly released Brenna's wrist, the fire dying out of his eyes. When he turned to Jason, Brenna recognized the tight smile on his face for what it was—a polite masking of his feelings. She'd seen it too often at the end of their marriage.

"You wouldn't want to run me by the hardware store in that nice car now, would you?" Jason cajoled, his blue eyes twinkling. "My brothers are going over to the fair and the missus has me stuck running errands."

"Well, if you promise not to make me help you set fenceposts again," Luke drawled teasingly, and Jason laughed.

"It's a deal! Might even buy you a cup of coffee for your trouble."

"All right," Luke agreed. "Be with you in a minute." He turned back to Brenna still standing at the counter and said in a neutral voice, "How about some donuts and coffee to go?" She started toward the kitchen door, but his voice arrested her. "Brenna," he said in a low tone, "I slept in the car last night." She looked back at him quickly, his eyes pinning her for a long second before he added, "Alone."

"Luke, I—" she began, but an apology seemed futile when she saw the steely curtain draw across his eyes again. "I'll get your coffee and donuts," she said wearily.

Loraine, who had been swiping a dishrag across the counter, came over to Brenna the instant the door closed behind Luke.

"And what was that all about?" she asked bluntly.

"Nothing," Brenna said, frowning down at the counter.

"He didn't come back to your house last night, did he?"

"If he didn't, I'm sure it's none of my concern," Brenna said, taking the rag and viciously attacking a coffee spill on the counter.

"Oh, I can see it doesn't bother you in the least," Loraine agreed mildly. "Any fool in here can see that from the scowl on your face, not to mention the fact that you're going to rub the top off that counter in about two seconds."

"We never could keep peace between us," Brenna said, putting down the rag and facing Loraine. "We're as different as night and day."

"Well, just remember that night and day have their dawn and dusk, and then they're not very different, after all." Loraine patted her shoulder. "There's more between you two than hard words, honey. Don't you remember the good times, too? I seem to recall how Luke used to bring you little presents all the time."

That made Brenna smile despite her mood. "He'd give me some silly little thing like a stick of gum and keep giving me little presents until he got to the real one."

"Well, you try to remember that, honey, every time that man makes you mad." Loraine glanced at her watch and sighed. "That's why God put men on earth anyway, to give women something to get mad at. It wouldn't surprise me if that serpent in the Garden of Eden was just something Adam made up to get Eve in trouble."

Brenna sighed. Loraine's logic didn't always follow clearcut rules, and Brenna had grown used to making her way through the thicket of twisted advice Loraine dispensed.

"You going over to the community center this afternoon?" Loraine asked.

"Oh, Lord, I almost forgot!" Brenna cried, breaking out of her trance. "I'd better get the spaghetti sauce started for you since I won't be around to help later." She darted toward the kitchen, stopping just long enough to glance over her shoulder and admonish Loraine. "And don't you dare go peeking into that Penney's bag."

Loraine, caught with her hand in midair, blushed and mumbled to herself tartly.

Much against Brenna's better judgment, Luke had insisted on coming to the Waldo Community Center with her. He tapped her gas gauge as he started the engine and grinned when it registered its usual half full.

He seemed to have forgotten about their words this morning, or else he was as determined as Brenna not to get into a fight.

"When did you start coming here?" he asked curiously as he pulled into the blacktop parking lot adjoining the old brick building that had once been an elementary school.

"Six or seven years ago," Brenna said, looking out at the bright construction-paper flowers taped on the windows. "The center was always short of volunteers, and I got together with some others who were interested and we made up a rotating schedule. I enjoy the children. They've filled a void in my life." When Luke didn't say anything, she dared a glance at him and found him studying her soberly.

"You wanted more children, didn't you, Brenna?" he asked at last, but she didn't want to answer that. That was dangerous ground and she wasn't ready to talk about it with Luke.

"Luke, I told you these kids aren't what you're used to. They have Down's syndrome. I'm sure you'll be bored. Go on back to the house and pick me up later."

"Don't decide for me what I want, Brenna," he said quietly.

"Fine," she said crisply. "Let's go in." He was being stubborn, she told herself. He was doing this to try to prove a point, a moot point as far as she was concerned. Maybe she didn't always know what he wanted, but she knew one thing about Luke McShane—what he wanted right this instant probably wasn't what he'd want two days or even two hours from now.

So Brenna's voice was a little tight and her spine stiff when she introduced Luke to Jeff Markert, the special-education teacher who ran the summer program for the kids. Brenna could see the wheels turning in Jeff's head as he glanced from one to the other. She knew he was wondering why she had never mentioned this ex-husband of hers. Jeff had moved to Waldo to take the teaching job, a move akin to marrying into a tightknit family and then spending years unraveling all the interpersonal relationships everyone else takes for granted.

A slight, fair man in his late twenties, Jeff had started a physical-education program for the children this summer, and now he was surrounded by ten excited, noisy children in shorts and T-shirts. "Everybody outside!" he ordered loudly, shooing them toward the back door and taking a firm grip on the whistle around his neck. "We'll start with warm-ups and then sprints today," he called to Brenna and Luke over the din.

Only one of the children, Eddie, was from Waldo. The others came from the surrounding area, from families starved for any organized program that would work with their children.

Outside, Brenna began dividing the kids into two teams for the sprints. She was about to ask Luke to supervise one team when she noticed a dark-haired young man walking around the school toward the field. Luke noticed him at the same time and said, "Be right back."

Brenna watched as he and the man greeted each other with a handshake and then conferred over something. Brenna issued automatic orders to the children, keeping half her attention concentrated on the two men. The stranger did most of the talking and Luke nodded solemnly, staring down at the ground, occasionally raising his eyes to scan the man's face. Finally Luke took a scrap of paper from his pocket, wrote something on it and handed it to the man. They shook hands again. The man left and Luke jogged back toward the group just as Elizabeth, a blond seven-year-old with a perpetual smile, broke away from the line and ran to him. Elizabeth's attention span was so brief that Brenna had nearly given up getting her to participate in the organized games. She would have gone after her, but one of the boys started to wander off, and he was easier to corral. Jeff had gone to the end of the field to act as the turning post and coach.

Jeff waved from his position down field, and Brenna looked over her two lines critically. "Now, when I say 'Go,' I want you to race as fast as you can to Jeff and then run back here to me. Then the next person in line will race. Okay?"

"I want to get my truck!" came a voice from near the end of the line. Brenna rushed to reassure Eddie that his truck was safe inside and would be waiting for him.

Satisfied that the children were temporarily under control, Brenna turned to look for Elizabeth. She was in Luke's arms and he was carrying her to the end of the line, engaged in an earnest discussion with her. Elizabeth's round face was focused on Luke, and for once her attention didn't lag. "We'll wait here at the end of the line for our turn, and then we'll run down to Jeff and back," he was telling her. "What do you think of that?" Elizabeth grinned back at him, and Luke knelt on the ground, cradling her between his legs.

Brenna's heart lurched at seeing them like that, Elizabeth's fair head close to Luke's dark one, his large hand gently holding the little girl's waist. It jolted Brenna back to the past and to the way she had imagined Luke would hold their own little girl. Her throat suddenly ached, and when Luke's eyes raised and met hers she could only stare helplessly. But she reminded herself that the stranger was a signal of some sort, a sign that Luke was even now being drawn away from here and from her life.

She turned away and hurried to the front of the line. She started the race somehow and encouraged the children to keep the goal in mind and to do their best. Each runner got a hug from her when he or she got back to the starting point.

Luke ran with Elizabeth, laughing and calling to her and keeping her going. Brenna's eyes followed them hungrily. He had to pick Elizabeth up and carry her the last few feet, and when they stopped in front of Brenna at last his eyes lit on her and grew pensive. "Are you all right?" he asked.

"Yes," she said at last. "Just a little hay fever." She produced a tissue from her pocket and rubbed her nose, but Luke didn't look convinced.

"I did good, didn't I?" Elizabeth crowed from his arms. Luke's attention was diverted, much to Brenna's relief.

"You did great, honey," he assured her, returning her wide grin.

"How many of you can touch your toes?" Brenna called, bringing the group to attention again. "Let me see." They were eager to show her, and she praised each one in turn, cajoling them into doing more toe touches for her. She could hear Luke talking to Elizabeth, making a game out of the toe touches and eliciting a laugh from her, but Brenna wouldn't look over her shoulder and watch them. There was too much danger in seeing Luke McShane like that, wrapped up in a little girl, his face unguarded.

Brenna waved to Charly Haywood as the young woman eased a van through the parking lot. "It looks like you really put them through their paces today!" Charly called as she leaned out the driver's window and smiled.

"We did our best!" Brenna assured her.

When the van was gone, Luke and Brenna got into her car and Brenna leaned her head back against the seat, tired but satisfied. Progress came in inches, not leaps, but it came nevertheless, and it never failed to move her when she saw a child master some new skill. Today it was Elizabeth finally completing a race, thanks to Luke.

"Isn't that van driver from Waldo?" Luke asked as he maneuvered the car onto the road.

Brenna nodded. "Eddie's her son. The summer program's only partially funded by the county and Charly couldn't afford the tuition, so she picks the kids up and takes them home to pay Eddie's way." She opened her eyes and glanced at Luke. "Not that Eddie would have been turned away, but Charly won't take a dime of anything she'd consider charity."

Luke nodded grimly. "Waldo should put up a statue in honor of its fiercely independent residents."

"And what's that supposed to mean?" Brenna asked, frowning.

Luke raked a hand through his dark hair and expelled a sharp breath. "Nothing." He sighed. "It's just frustrating to see kids like that who need help so desperately."

"There's state money to hire another person besides Jeff," Brenna said, "but you can imagine how hard it is to get someone with a degree to come to a place like Waldo. We had a young woman early last year, but she got a better offer and moved on."

Luke nodded shortly, and Brenna looked out the window at the passing fields and telephone poles. That was the problem—people always seemed to move on from Waldo. And Luke was no exception.

"You hungry?" he asked, pulling into the Dairy Delight that catered to the high school crowd. "Let's take some hamburgers home."

It was a place they used to come to a lot when they were in high school, and even later when they were married. Like the Chestnut Tree Cafe, it had never changed. Begun in the fifties by a retired schoolteacher, taken over later by his son and daughter-in-law, the Dairy Delight refused to bow to change.

"Two Elvis Burgers with everything?" Luke asked, digging in his pocket for his wallet.

Brenna nodded, watching him go inside and thinking how provincial Waldo must appear to him. For the first time, she began to understand why he had felt the need to go away. He probably hadn't run across a single Elvis Burger anywhere else in the country.

They took the bag of food back to the house and sat on the front steps, quietly eating the burgers, along with the Blue Suede Shoestring Fries and the All Shook Up Shakes. Brenna was growing more depressed by the moment.

"I saw Frank Hargrove when I was getting the burgers," Luke said. "I think he was trying to insure the Dairy Delight against food poisoning."

Brenna punched his arm, but she grinned nevertheless.

"Ow!" But he grinned, too. "What's with his eyebrows anyway?" Luke asked after another bite of his burger. "They always looked like two caterpillars crossing a highway, but he's done something to them."

"He dyes his hair and he does his eyebrows to match," Brenna said.

"Yeah?"

"Mmm-hmm. The color never comes out the same, though. The Conley brothers swear you can predict the weather by Frank's eyebrows. If they're dark, we're in for a hard winter with lots of snow. If they're on the blond side, you can plant your potatoes by mid-March."

"No kidding? Those Conley brothers always did get the best yields of any farmers around here. On the way to the hardware store today, Jason said they're going to invest in a new combine this year and they're paying cash. They're one of the few farms making it these days."

"Luke, don't feel you have to make polite conversation about Waldo for my benefit," Brenna said suddenly, crumpling the paper from her burger and dropping it into the bag.

When she glanced at him, she saw he was watching her with a solemn light in his eyes. "What's wrong, Brenna?"

"Nothing. I guess I'm just tired." She turned away, but his hand touched her face, fingers curling under her jaw, bringing her back around to face him. His touch was cool and gentle, and it sent shock waves of longing through her.

"Don't do that," he said quietly. "Don't turn away like that, Brenna. Talk to me."

"Luke, there's nothing to talk about."

"Yes, there is, Brenna! For God's sake, let's stop hiding from each other! We're not kids anymore. Let's at least try to communicate." His hand left her jaw, fingers trailing slightly down her neck before he withdrew his touch, leaving her feeling bereft. "Talk to me, Brenna. Please."

She took a deep, shaky breath, her skin remembering his touch the way the sand holds a footprint. "I hardly know you anymore, Luke," she said softly. "Maybe I never did. I don't even know where to begin."

"Anything," he prompted her gently, blue eyes skimming her face restlessly, coming to rest on her mouth. "Start with anything, Brenna. But let's stop being strangers."

The word *strangers* reminded her of the man at the school that afternoon and she frowned. "All right," she said tentatively. "Who was that man who came to see you today?"

"A client from Iowa," Luke said immediately, catching her gaze and holding it.

"A client?"

He nodded. "I've been working with the racing circuit there, setting up a kind of support group for the racers, mechanics, anybody's who's interested. Harry, the guy you saw today, has a drug problem. He's not directly connected with the circuit, but he likes the races. He's kind of a hanger-on. He was friends with a driver who...who died." His eyes slid away from hers, and Brenna could feel his openness sliding away, too.

"You set up this program yourself?" she asked hesitantly.

Luke shrugged. "I saw the need." He was looking down her drive now, toward the road, his eyes focused on something Brenna was sure didn't include her. "Track people get to be like family, and like families they have their own problems. The trouble was, the way people have to travel around the circuit, they need a support group of their own, one that can follow them from track to track." He scratched his chin absently, glancing at her sideways. "I finished my degree a few years ago, in sociology. But I guess you knew that."

"Denny didn't say... I mean, I didn't know what you studied." Trust a younger brother not to tell the things she really wanted to know, she thought in irritation.

Luke was waiting, as though he expected her to say something else, but she didn't. Finally he stood and stretched, then bent to pick up the bag with their discarded paper. "I guess I'll go in and get cleaned up. The baseball game's on the radio tonight. I might listen to it in the bedroom."

Brenna nodded as he went in. She wanted to tell him he could listen to it in the kitchen with her, but she couldn't find the words. Things were still too tentative between them, too much like old lace, so fragile it might crumble at the slightest touch.

She sat on the porch awhile longer, and when she was sure he was in the bathroom she went to her car, unlocked the trunk and took out the Penney's bag she'd stowed there that afternoon.

She sat up, disoriented, when she heard the crash. For a moment she thought it was ten years ago and she had fallen asleep waiting for Luke to come home from the track. But the ten years were gone and the crash had come from the bedroom she and Luke used to share, she realized as she came fully awake. She rubbed her hand over her temple wearily. Nothing like an Elvis Burger to promote a troubled sleep.

There was another thud from the room, less loud, and then a muffled groan. Brenna slid out from the sheet and started for the door, her heart hammering. She stopped in the hall, seeing no lights on in his room and she realized she was wearing a short, lacy nightgown, the kind Luke would have approved of when they were married.

It was crazy, absolutely devoid of logic, but she had taken to buying nightgowns like these the last two years, as though to compensate for something that was lost to her. She half froze to death in them in winter, but somehow they were a kind of lifeline, an affirmation that the woman in her hadn't died with her baby.

This particular gown ended midthigh and was all pink swirls and beige lace. The straps and cups were almost entirely lace and afforded a generous view of pale flesh beneath. Brenna started back to her room to fetch a robe, but a dim light came on in Luke's room and she went there instead, drawn inexorably to it and to Luke.

The light seeping from under the door made her sad, and she realized that after Dory died she had left that light on often while waiting up for Luke, waiting for some end to the torment they both felt.

Gently she pushed open the door, her heart catching in her throat when she saw him sitting on the edge of the bed in his undershorts, his head in his hands. A picture frame lay facedown on the floor, shards of glass scattered around it.

"Luke, are you all right?" she asked softly, her voice sounding strange to her.

He glanced up and the haunted misery in his eyes made her take a step back. "Go back to bed, Brenna. I just had a bad dream."

"Let me pick this up," she said, needing to be useful and needing to be near him a little longer to make sure he really was all right. She knelt on the floor, gingerly picking up pieces of glass, and Luke immediately squatted down beside her.

"You'll cut yourself," he said. "Let me do that." His voice wasn't harsh, just infinitely weary, as though he'd traveled a long distance and was badly in need of rest.

He reached up to the nightstand, got the newspaper he must have been reading when he went to bed and scooped the glass onto it. His large bronzed hands moved swiftly and efficiently, and he wouldn't look at her.

Luke turned the picture over and set it back on the stand. Brenna's eyes followed it and saw that it was a picture of her that her father had taken in front of the café about three years ago. It was the café's anniversary, and Fergie had insisted on a celebration, complete with cake and banners—and free bran muffins to all customers. In the picture Brenna was grinning and holding a coffeepot. It was one of her father's favorite pictures, and it had been sitting on the chest of drawers on the other side of the room. She dimly registered that Luke must have moved the picture for obscure reasons of his own.

Luke shoved the newspaper and shards into the wastepaper basket and stood, rubbing his hand over his eyes before he sat down on the edge of the bed. Brenna couldn't take her eyes off him and she remained kneeling on the floor, hardly feeling the rough abrasion of the wooden boards.

He raised his eyes to look at her, and his mouth opened slightly, but no words came out. Instead he slowly extended his hand to her. Without thought Brenna took it. She could feel his fingers trembling and she went to him quickly and without reservation. She stood between his legs, his hand still clasping hers tightly.

Her other hand wavered in the air only an instant before she let it dip into the luxurious thick black hair, now disheveled by sleep. His eyes met hers and his need was painfully apparent. At that moment Brenna would have done anything for him, anything to take away the pain he was feeling.

He managed a shaky smile as he looked at her. "Is this from your Penney's bag?" he murmured, his voice sounding hoarse.

Brenna shook her head, forcing a smile for him, a smile that faded. "No. Another one of my impulse purchases."

"I like it," he said. "Brenna..." But he didn't finish the sentence, pulling her to him instead and putting his arm behind her legs to lift her and settle her in his lap. His arms cradled and caressed her, his fingers still trembled.

"My God, but you're even more beautiful," he said in awe. She looked into his face and saw something she'd mourned for so many years. It was like opening a door in an abandoned house and finding something precious you thought so lost it could never be retrieved.

Luke buried his head in her neck, breathing raggedly, as though starved for the feel of her. His hand slid up her body, over the silken sea of her nightgown and cupped her breast. He caressed and stroked, and Brenna thought she must be dreaming. This pleasure couldn't exist in ordinary, waking life. Her head fell back against his arm and her breath escaped in a sound that was like desire caught on the wind.

Luke's thumb hooked brazenly under a shoulder strap and tugged. The lace slid effortlessly from her shoulder and she felt languid summer air flutter over her bare skin an instant before Luke's mouth took her breast. Brenna arched against that touch, that searing male desire so blatant in the feverish strokes of his tongue and in the hardness pressing her hip.

Her nipples tightened almost painfully in their need to be touched by Luke. Her body ached for him, and yet she felt a desolate need to cry. This was desire. This was a physical hunger that threatened to tear her apart with its urgency. And yet there was something more she needed, something indefinable, something she was afraid Luke McShane could never give her.

His hand tightened in her hair and he raised his head to look into her face, as if summoned by her thoughts. Whatever demons had awakened him and made him knock the picture to the floor were gone now, beaten back into the depths of Luke's soul. His eyes burned with another hunger.

But whatever was on her face stilled him. His gaze moved restlessly over her, and then the darkness softened and she saw regret and sadness etch themselves there.

"It's late," he whispered hoarsely, putting her gently back on her feet. "You'd better get some sleep."

His hands are still trembling, she thought in wild distraction, torn between wanting to touch him again and wanting to flee from the desire still welling up in her.

She hesitated a second, then pulled up her strap and hurried from the room. The physical need was still there between them. It was a raging hunger that ten years had done nothing to diminish, but something else was still missing, some bond they had never managed to forge. When Brenna slipped between her cool sheets she found herself on the verge of tears for what they had never had.

Staring up at the ceiling in his own room, Luke cursed himself for coming so close to making love to her. Only the puzzled sadness in her face had stopped him. He had never intended on hurting her when he came back, and tonight he had nearly done just that.

Five

———

Brenna started for the stairs, her arms full of freshly laundered sheets that smelled faintly of the honeysuckle that grew near the clothesline. She stopped to look out the west window where the sun had baked the sky a boiling red and stained the clouds to ginger peach at the edges. It hadn't rained in the two weeks since Brenna had gone to Luke's room when he knocked over the picture.

Luke had fixed the frame and glass the next day, and she couldn't help noticing that the picture still sat on the nightstand beside his bed. But there had been no mention of what had happened, of how she had ended up in his arms. And he had been very careful not to touch her since then. She could see the wariness in his eyes and in the shifting of his arms slightly away from her whenever they happened to stand close to each other. And it pained her.

She heard an engine and saw his car turn into her drive, kicking up small clouds of dust. She turned away and went on up the stairs to his room.

She had no idea what he did. Sometimes he was gone before she even got up in the morning. And often he didn't return until late at night. She knew he spent a lot of time with Avery at Custom Rebuilding, but other than that his comings and goings were a mystery to her.

This was a cold echo from their marriage, she thought bitterly as she spread the bottom sheet on the bed and began pulling the corners over the mattress. Years ago she would lie in bed alone at night and feel the aching need for him spread to every inch of her being until she thought she would turn to ashes from it. A word, a touch, a look—it was always the simple things women craved, she'd decided, things that were so easy to give unless you were a man who wanted race tracks more.

She snapped the top sheet in the air and watched it settle onto the bed in furrows and peaks. Her life had settled into a pattern like that, folds and crevices here and there, one texture and one shade. She had little secrets she kept just for herself—her lacy nightgowns and her wisteria vine that she watered weekly and implored to bloom every spring, in futility it seemed. The wisteria had disappointed her for ten years now, and she supposed that life had done the same.

"Can I help you?"

She hadn't heard him come in the house or go up the stairs and his voice made her jump. "No," she said, turning around. "I'm almost done."

"Let me get the other side." He didn't wait for her permission. He just rounded the bed and began straightening the sheet and tucking in the end. Brenna found her eyes lingering on his fingers as they smoothed the sheet, wondering at the ease with which he dispensed with the tangles. Why was it, she asked herself, that a woman always expected a man to straighten out the wrinkles in her life?

Together they pulled up the comforter, then he stood watching her as she pulled the pillowcases over the pillows. She always felt sad when he watched her like this, as though Luke saw all the tiny holes in the fabric of her life.

"Are you hungry?" she asked, her hands stilling on the pillow as she held it to her. He looked tired—he always looked tired lately—and there was a smudge of grease on his forehead.

He shook his head. "I'll eat later. I want to go see Dad before it gets too late. I was there this morning, but he was sleeping."

He came around the bed, not looking into her face though she willed him to, and started for the door.

"Luke," she said hesitantly, halting him though he didn't turn around. "I'd like to go with you."

He did look at her then, and the lonely man that was Luke McShane was reflected in his eyes like the moon over a river. His eyes were so blue and restless and filled with some unnameable longing. Did he want to be gone from this place and from her? Is that what she was seeing?

"I can deal with this, Brenna," he said, not unkindly. "You don't have to go."

"I want to go," she said, forgetting her pride for the moment. "I care very much for your father, too."

He acquiesced with a barely perceptible nod, and Brenna slowly laid the pillow on the bed and followed him.

James's voice was a slow, tired murmur as he talked to Luke. Brenna watched father and son, Luke sitting on the edge of the bed, the almost foggy hospital light sifting over his face and turning it dusky and weary. His hand held his father's, carefully avoiding the intravenous tube.

James was giving Luke instructions, haltingly and between labored intakes of breath, about some possessions he'd left with his former landlord. Luke was nodding, his eyes crystal chips of sadness.

Feeling as though she was intruding on something private, Brenna stood quietly and slipped out the door. Leaning against the cool wall outside, she took a deep, steadying breath.

"Are you all right?" someone asked solicitously, and Brenna looked up to see Julie, the nurse she had met the first time she came here with Luke, standing in front of her holding a water pitcher.

"Yes," Brenna said, making an effort to smile. "I thought they needed some time alone."

Julie nodded and studied Brenna. She looked over her shoulder as another nurse walked by and said, "Ann, would you take this to Mrs. Hawkins in 203?" She handed the water pitcher to the nurse and turned back to Brenna.

"How's Luke holding up?" she asked.

Brenna ran a hand through her hair before she answered, "He's exhausted. And he doesn't talk about it."

Julie pursed her lips thoughtfully. "He really needs you now," she said.

Brenna shook her head emphatically. "Luke McShane's never needed anyone in his life. Give him a race track and a fast car, and he can weather any storm."

"I don't think so," Julie said carefully. "I see people all the time when they have someone they love in the hospital, and it makes them try to be strong for everyone else. They end up wearing themselves out with the pretending."

That was Luke—strong. And Brenna didn't know how much of it was really pretending for her benefit and for James. "Julie," she said slowly. "James is very sick, isn't he?"

Julie looked at the floor before she met Brenna's eyes. "That's up to Luke to tell you," she said. She squeezed Brenna's shoulder and hurried on down the hall, but Brenna had her answer. She wondered if Luke would go on shouldering this all himself, or if for once in his life he would let her share his pain.

"I have a present for you," he said on the way home in the car. Brenna glanced at him. He was looking straight ahead and he appeared somber, his eyes as dark as the indigo sky.

"Oh," Brenna said, unsure how to respond. The lines around his eyes were tight, as though his emotions were pulled taut beneath his skin.

Luke cast her a wry sideways glance. "'Oh?' That's not what you're supposed to say. Don't you remember?"

And then she knew that he was playing their old game. *I have a present for you.* "Excuse me," she said formally. "Where's my present?"

"'Where's my present?'" he repeated with a great show of pretended outrage. "No, no. You're supposed to say, 'I can't guess what it is.'"

Brenna rolled her eyes.

"Well, come on."

"What?"

"Say it."

Brenna sighed. "I can't guess what it is," she said, less than enthusiastically.

Grinning now, Luke reached into his pocket and dropped a dull-colored penny into her hand.

"What's this?" Brenna said, frowning.

"No, no! You're supposed to say, 'Just what I wanted.'" Luke gave her a mild elbow in the ribs and a teasing raise of his eyebrows.

"Just what I wanted," she parroted, turning the penny over in her hand and inspecting the date.

Luke beamed. "I found it in the café parking lot."

"Well, that *is* impressive," she said dryly. The penny was nine years old. She wasn't sure she wanted to play this game anymore, but Luke was apparently just getting warmed up.

"I have another present for you," he said.

"Really," Brenna began, stopping when his eyebrows twitched again. He was doing this to take his mind off James, she decided, and she would play along. "I can't guess what it is," she said dutifully.

"There you go," Luke said, grinning as he dropped a button into her hand.

"My, my," she said, inspecting the tiny white button with red dots. It looked like something from a child's sweater, and she resolutely forced that thought from her mind. "From the parking lot again, no doubt," she said, then added, "Just what I wanted."

Luke was turning the car into Brenna's drive, simultaneously pulling something from his shirt pocket, something he dangled in front of her between thumb and forefinger.

"Oooooo," Brenna murmured appreciatively as she snatched the chocolate bar. "Now this *is* just what I wanted. And I don't want to hear about it if it's from the parking lot."

"I would not give you a used candy bar," he said, pretending to be wounded by her lack of confidence.

"You gave me a used penny and a used button," she pointed out as she unwrapped the candy.

"By the way," he said, stopping the car and turning to face her. "I have another present for you."

She halted in midbite and studied him. He was serious now, though he was trying not to show it, giving her a crooked smile and a shrug instead. This next one was the big present, the last in the series. She remembered the game and how it had always ended. The last present was given and she and Luke ended up in bed, laughing and kissing.

"I don't know," she said, looking down and trying to make her voice light. "I'm already overwhelmed by the candy bar."

Long fingers gently lifted her chin. "If you don't want it, it's okay."

She searched his face, looking for answers she hadn't found in ten years, answers she never would find. She wanted to know why things happened, why her life felt so still, like the baby she'd carried inside her body, why her heart could ache so just from the look of Luke's face. But they were answers she could never have. What she could

have now was Luke's present, and the sadness in his eyes
made her want not to hurt him.

"I'd like my present," she said hesitantly.

He didn't make her say the right words this time, just
grinned and leaped from the car, opening her door and
pulling her along with him toward the garage.

"Did you get me a new car?" she asked hopefully. He
gave her a quelling glance over his shoulder. "Now, what
kind of present would that be?" he asked.

"A darn good one," Brenna sighed.

It took her eyes a few seconds to adjust when he halted
just inside the dark, cool garage. Brenna looked around
curiously. He had been cleaning up things in here, she noticed. The rake, hoe and snow shovel now hung neatly on
wall pegs, the gas-powered weed trimmer sported a new roll
of cutting string—something Brenna had meant to do all last
summer while the weeds behind the garage grew to Califor-
nia-redwood heights—and the lawn mower sat gleaming in
a shaft of light from the window, the metal housing obviously recently cleaned.

Brenna nodded toward the mower. "It doesn't work.
Hasn't since last month."

"That's because there was a clod of dirt as big as Pitts-
burgh stuck on the blades. What did you do, try to mow a
wheat field?" Shaking his head, he gently turned her toward the corner of the room. "Your present's over there,"
he said, pointing.

A board? He got her a big board? She squinted and
frowned, then moved closer. A headboard. It was a bed's
headboard. Slowly she reached out her hand to touch the
ornamental trim at the top, the curlicues and spools, and
something stirred in her memory.

"Don't you remember it?" he said, coming to stand beside her. "It's from that little motel in Iowa where we spent
our honeymoon. I was racing up there last year and they
were about to tear down the motel, so I went over and
bought the headboard from Room 10. Hell, the same own-

ers were there. Remember them? The retired couple? They're moving to Florida.'' He stopped abruptly as Brenna quickly withdrew her hand from the wood as though it had burst into flames. "Brenna?'' he asked quizzically. "What's wrong? Did you forget about it? You loved that headboard so much. I...thought you'd like to have it. I refinished it for you.''

Room 10. Their honeymoon. The old couple. It was too much. Nothing tangible from their past had existed when Luke came back, but now there was this. The headboard of the bed where they'd lain together, had fueled each other's passions and dreams, had promised that life would yield all its riches for them because they were so blessed. They had said they would grow old together like the couple who owned the motel and had been married for almost fifty years. How could she forget any of that? And how could he so wrenchingly bring the past back to her?

"Why, Luke?'' she demanded, her voice as soft and ghostly as the dusting of cobwebs in the high corner of the garage. "Why did you have to come back here?'' Tears filling her eyes, she turned and ran for the house, hearing his bewildered voice behind her. He kept calling her name, but he stopped in the kitchen when she ran on up the stairs to her room and threw herself on the bed.

The tears flowed freely now, and she let them fall on the bedspread and pillow, holding her fist to her mouth to keep from sobbing. And when the tears finally ceased, she admitted to herself that Luke McShane had succeeded in breaking through that fragile shell she cloaked herself in. He'd gotten to her this time, and the stillness of her life was broken like glass.

The room was dark when Brenna woke up and she glanced at the clock. Midnight. It was oppressively hot and a thin sheen of perspiration covered her skin. The window was open; slivers of quicksilver lightning lit the sky in the distance.

Brenna was stiff from lying in the same position so long. She slowly sat up and began peeling off her blouse and slacks. The hall was dark; there was no light from Luke's room as she padded barefoot in her underwear to the bathroom. She washed quickly in the sink, dropping her underwear to the floor and running the washcloth and soap over her warm skin. She didn't use a towel, just slipped back down the hall to her bedroom, letting the summer air dry her bare skin.

With a pang she remembered what she had said when he had given her the headboard and she stopped at her doorway, frowning. There was a faint light flickering downstairs and she could hear a soft whirring. Luke was up late again. She decided she ought to tell him now she was sorry for what she said about him coming back. It was just that the headboard had made her hurt in a way she didn't think he could understand.

She didn't want to turn on a light, so she just groped in her drawer for a robe and came up with something short and soft. It was her pink silk robe that came only to midthigh. But she was in a hurry and it would have to do. She slid it on and tied it at the waist. Then she pushed her hair back from her face and padded downstairs.

The light was coming from the living room and Brenna stopped hesitantly at the foot of the stairs when she realized what it was. Luke must have found their old movie projector in the closet and now he was running it. It had been so long ago when they'd bought the camera—before the days of camcorders—that Brenna couldn't even remember what was on the films they'd taken. The house, she supposed, and Luke's trophies. Her father had spliced the films together years ago, so they were on one big reel.

Silently she moved to the living room, coming to a dazed stop as she rounded the corner. The projector was resting on two catalogs on the low coffee table, sending its beam of light to the opposite wall. Brenna's eyes followed the light, unwilling captive of what she was seeing. There, flickering on her faded wallpaper, was her brief marriage with Luke, suddenly come to life again in this room. There was Luke with James, each of them with an arm around the other's shoulder, grinning and waving their paint brushes at the camera. It must have been the day they painted the front porch. Brenna remembered how proud they were of their handiwork when they finished. While they were still admiring it, the barnyard cat had brought a mouse up the steps and released it on the freshly painted porch while they all watched. The cat and mouse pawprints were visible for years.

There was Luke holding up a trophy, leaning on his red racer and grinning cockily. He looked so young—and so happy. Somebody else took the camera and there they all were, washing Luke's car: James, Brenna's father, Luke, Brenna, even Loraine. Denny was home then, Brenna realized, when she saw him stand up from behind the car and aim the hose at the feet of the person holding the camera. Brenna knew it must be Denny's wife taking the pictures. This was so long ago, before Denny's wife divorced him and before... Luke left.

Time rolled on, and now Brenna was in the kitchen baking something, talking to the camera and obviously trying to make whoever was taking the pictures—Luke, no doubt—get out from underfoot. She turned around in mock exasperation, brandishing a rolling pin, and Brenna sucked in her breath when she saw herself eight months pregnant.

Unconsciously she touched her stomach, feeling only a flatness there, an emptiness under the shroudlike softness of her robe. In that instant she would have sold her soul to relive one of those days with Luke McShane, just one day from dawn to sunset and then the night, when Brenna felt as though she was a part of the world and not some quiet, forgotten child watching it glide past her.

She must have made a sound, a groan, or her robe rustled, and she caught a shadowy movement in the huge upholstered chair by the window. She knew that in the dark Luke was now watching her and not her image on the wall.

She didn't move, hardly dared to breathe. Her eyes were beginning to pick out his silhouette in the chair when lightning flashed, briefly illuminating the window and etching Luke's face before the room sank back into shadow. *He was crying.* She'd seen the tears on his face, the pain in his eyes, the lonely slump of his shoulders before night closed in again. She'd seen Luke McShane when he was finally vulnerable, and now she trembled with the need to touch him.

Please, her heart cried. Just one sign, one small sign that you need me. Don't push me away.

Each breath ached in her throat as she waited in the humid darkness, hearing only the steady purr of the projector and the deep whispers of approaching thunder.

It felt like an eternity before he spoke.

"Brenna...will you...sit with me? Just for a little while." His voice might have been the thunder; it sounded so far away, so like a phantom. But it had been real, and he had asked her to stay. Her body tremulous with emotion, she glided silently to the chair.

He caught her hand, twined his fingers with hers and pulled her onto his lap. He brought her head to his chest and she felt his heartbeat quicken beneath her cheek as he stroked her hair. His chest was bare and the feel of his smooth, hard skin and the springy dark hair covering it made her want to cry with want. Why was it that she never got enough of the feel of Luke? A touch made her crave another touch, and still that wasn't enough, and in the fraction of a second it took lightning to flash she wanted the entire man, Luke McShane, her dark, handsome racer, wanted every inch of his body claiming her. She was almost shaking with wanting him, but she forced herself not to let him know. She had schooled herself into hiding her feelings from him, and old habits died hard.

"It feels like it was only yesterday," he whispered. "I see you there and I see Dad and I think everything's the same. Only it isn't."

"Don't," she whispered back, caressing his chest with her palm. "Don't hurt yourself like this." Instinctively she knew he was blaming himself for what had happened, and she couldn't let him shoulder that kind of guilt. She sensed something else, too, something he was trying to keep from telling her.

"I-I almost came to your room tonight," he began haltingly. "To talk to you, to ask you to sit with me awhile. But I've been alone for so long I didn't even know how to do it, how to ask you that. It seemed an incredibly hard thing to do."

"I know," she murmured. "I told you the other day that our hearts had frozen, and I think they had. When I saw you sitting in the dark I wanted to come touch you, but I couldn't remember how I should do it. Isn't that terrible? To forget something as necessary as how to touch another human being. There are fairy tales about statues and puppets brought to life, but I think I did the opposite. I think I turned to stone."

"No," Luke said hoarsely, his breath warm against her hair. "Not you. You're the most caring woman I've ever known. That's why I think I had to...come see you again." He took a deep breath and Brenna could feel a trembling in his hands. She braced herself for what he would say. "I needed you, Brenna," he said quietly. "Dad's dying."

She raised her head quickly and saw the shadows and pain in his eyes. "Oh, God," she whispered, closing her eyes, feeling the hot tears gather there.

"He was feeling tired and weak a couple of years ago and he went in for a checkup," Luke said wearily. "They found leukemia then, and they got it in remission. But . . . it came back. And they can't stop it this time."

"Luke, I'm so—" She didn't get the rest out because her own tears choked her throat. Blindly she reached up a hand

and touched his cheek, felt his tears on her fingers and let
her own fall onto his bare skin. Another loss they had to
endure. She wondered if they would find themselves powerless to comfort each other again this time.

They sat that way a long time, hearing the thunder rum-
ble closer while their ghostly twins from the past wavered on
the wall. When their tears were spent they just held each
other.

The wind picked up as the storm drew closer. Luke
shifted. "Brenna," he said softly, but she heard the need in
his voice. "Go back to bed now, honey." When she didn't
move, his fingers sifted through her hair and a hard sigh escaped him. "I'm not very strong, Brenna," he murmured.
"You're going to have to say no for both of us." He stood
up with her in his arms and moved as if to set her on her
feet, but he didn't. He couldn't seem to stop looking at her.
His eyes devoured her face and hair and the milky skin
showing beneath the skimpy robe. "Brenna," he groaned.

She couldn't answer his plea because she couldn't tear her
eyes away from him, either. Her arms tightened around his
neck and Luke whispered her name hoarsely again.

"Tell me to go away, honey," he said tightly. "I don't
want to hurt you any more than I have."

But she couldn't do that any more than she could tell her
heart to stop aching for him. Instead she let her head fall
back against his arm, her hair sweeping down in a tangle of
tawny waves, and she looked boldly into his face. Even in
the dark she could read the hunger there. Lightning lit the
room for one silvery instant and Luke's eyes blazed with
unconcealed need.

"Brenna, I—" he began, and then he groaned and said
her name again, investing it with the pain and loneliness
they'd both felt in the last ten years. Gently he knelt on the
braided rug by the chair, reaching up to pull down the blue-
and-white afghan and lay it under her. Her robe fell open at
the top, and her skin, her hair and the pink silk robe bor-

rowed a pearly sheen from the projector's glow, as though the past was sending out a faint light of its own.

Luke bent over her. Her name was on his lips, and then he lowered his lips to her feverish skin, melding the word with her own body like a brand. "Brenna," he whispered against her neck, then again in the hollow between her breasts and at last softly on the aching tip of one breast, taut and straining toward him.

The warm, moist ministrations of his tongue sent her groaning and writhing beneath him, and his hand fueled her passion as callused fingers, incredibly gentle when the need arose, played patterns on the tender skin of her thighs. He was the sun of her world, and she wanted his heat and energy and burning touch. Luke McShane, as dark as ebony in the shadowed room, was like a dream lover come to possess her with the past.

The storm drew closer with its swirls of writhing light, its booming cadence of clouds clashing. A gust of cool wind blew open the front door and rattled the screen against the frame. The air rushed over them with the fury of demon breath, but they were lost in each other's passion, their own storm rivaling anything outside.

The need to touch this dark lover of hers overwhelmed Brenna, and she greedily explored the hard muscles of his back and chest with her hands as he suckled her, driving her toward a sea of pleasure in which she would surely drown. Her fingers shook as she fumbled with his belt and snap, but finally she had his jeans undone. A groan was wrenched from him as her hand sought and found the hardness of him there.

Luke levered himself onto one elbow and kicked off his shoes, then his jeans and underwear. He was so beautiful, she thought, with his lean body, each muscle etched in steel. He pulled her robe all the way open and took a sharp inhalation as his eyes moved over her.

Her hands sought to relearn each edge and hollow of his body, to satisfy a hunger that had lain waiting for ten years.

Brenna touched and stroked, remembering the sensitive skin of his flanks, her fingernails lightly caressing there, eliciting a husky groan. Her fingertips skimmed his flat nipples, delved into the dark hair on his chest and then followed it down lower to where it feathered into black down. Her tongue followed her fingers until strong hands closed on her arms and brought her back to the afghan and under the scrutiny of fiery blue eyes.

"If you're trying to drive me crazy, you're doing an excellent job," he murmured on a ragged breath. "Did I tell you I love that robe?" His smile was as devilish as his eyes as he quickly divested her of the robe. "Is this what was in your Penney's bag?"

She shook her head, her smile letting him know she had other secrets he would like, as well. She suddenly felt as alluring as a siren luring men to her lair. Never in her life did she feel irresistible—unless she was in Luke's arms.

"You're going to tease me, are you?" he whispered, his smile widening. Then he proceeded to tease her with his lips and fingers until she was nearly incoherent with desire. She couldn't speak, could only watch the pleasure on his face as her eyes widened and her mouth formed a soft round O. His knee gently nudged open her legs as his mouth claimed hers with a ferocity that left no doubt that he was as impatient for her as she was for him.

"Luke," she murmured hesitantly when he lifted his mouth and brushed back her hair with trembling fingers. She wanted him so much that she hurt physically.

"What is it, honey?"

"Luke, I haven't... There hasn't been...since you." Her eyes caught his and held.

He understood, and gentle fingers brushed her softly. "It's all right," he assured her, kissing her mouth again. "We'll go slow." He gave her a crooked smile. "At least I'll try to go slow, honey."

He entered her then, and Brenna felt his possession as a completion she'd been denied for too long. The sheer pleasure made her arch her back, and his anxious eyes scanned her face, afraid he'd hurt her. Brenna shook her head. "No... no... it's just so good."

He was slow at first, but Brenna found she didn't want slow. She wanted Luke McShane the way she'd had him in the past, all driving muscles and demanding male, and she showed him what she wanted, nipping at his neck and urgently running her hands down his back.

"Brenna!" he rasped. "Honey, you don't know what you're doing to me." He raised his head, dark fair falling rakishly onto his forehead and when he saw her face, the sparks in his eyes grew into flames. "All right, honey," he growled. "The hell with slow."

The sheen of moisture on their bodies glowed in the flickering light of their past dancing across the wall. The wind swirled around and over them, riffling magazines on the coffee table and flipping the ends of the crocheted doilies under the vases. Thunder cracked and the room glowed with lightning flashes, one following on the heels of the last. Rain pelted the roof and windows, slowly at first, with heavy thuds, and then with a squall of wind and pouring water.

But Luke and Brenna were locked in a storm of their own. Nothing existed outside of them and the maelstrom of pleasure holding them at its vortex. Brenna felt every nerve tightened to the point of breaking, pushing her, pushing her... And then the incredible waves of pleasure swept through her, rippled through every part of her body and left her spent and almost senseless. She lay on her back, her body cooling in the influx of damp wind as Luke used his mouth to dry the drops of moisture from her.

He was gone from her momentarily, turning off the projector and closing the front door, and then he was back, rearranging the afghan and cradling her exhausted body against his.

She slept deeply and peacefully for the first time in years, coming awake sometime before dawn, feeling desire rising in her again. When she looked at Luke she found that he was awake, too, watching her, and when he smiled she knew that the storm would carry them away again.

Six

Seems to me you must've done some heavy lifting to make your back so sore," Loraine observed as Brenna leaned against the counter and flexed her torso, wincing. "Or maybe it was something else," Loraine concluded, pursing her lips curiously.

It was spending the night on a hardwood floor with only an afghan and Luke for padding that had put the crick in Brenna's back, but Brenna wasn't about to tell Loraine that. When she had awakened this morning the afghan was tucked around her, a pillow was under her head and Luke was gone. She'd spent most of today wondering just how much he regretted what had happened last night.

"You need me to pop your backbone for you?" Fergie asked as he came from the kitchen carrying a tray with the three rhubarb pies Brenna had made two hours ago.

"No, she don't want her back popped," Loraine answered for her. "She's in no mood to be messed with. Best let sleeping dogs make their own beds."

"Let sleeping dogs lie," Brenna corrected her automatically.

"Huh?" Loraine said, getting that look in her eye that said she wasn't in any mood to be trifled with.

"Naw," Fergie threw in as he deftly sliced the pies. "It's 'The early dog gets the fleas.' "

"I think I know what my own grandmother used to say," Loraine insisted, clearly peeved. "And that wasn't it."

Sighing, Brenna poured herself a glass of iced tea and sat down in the booth by the window. It was almost four and the café was empty. The supper crowd would arrive right on schedule at five. That was the problem around here, Brenna thought. Everything went according to schedule. You even had to schedule your appetite. Funny that that had never bothered her before.

"If you don't feel like talking, that's all right," Loraine said, sitting down opposite her with a cup of coffee. " 'Cause you know I'm never at a loss for words."

Brenna couldn't help smiling. That was true, although the words sometimes got mangled. "I'm all right," she said.

"Sure you are," Loraine said. "You always tell everyone you're all right, my girl. But I've been around you enough to know when you got the blue devils. Now, you want to say anything about it, or should I just go yell at Fergie for putting oat bran in the biscuits?"

Brenna's smile faded and she stared down at the table. "Luke's dad's dying," she said softly.

"That's a hard thing to do anything about," Loraine said gently. "He hasn't been so good for a while, has he?"

Brenna shook her head.

"And Luke?" Loraine probed.

"He's dealing with it," Brenna said succinctly.

Loraine made a thoughtful humming sound. "And you wouldn't, by chance, have helped him 'deal with it,' so to speak?"

When Brenna glanced up, she found Loraine studying her with her sharp bird's eyes, no doubt having come to her own conclusions as to why Brenna's back was out of whack today. "I'm afraid I...may have gotten a little too involved," Brenna put it delicately. "Luke was looking for a little comfort, and we...well, things happened."

Loraine rolled her eyes. "Lord, child, you young people think too much! It's probably because you were all raised according to that Dr. Spock's baby book, and all because your mamas felt they didn't know enough on their own. Well, let me tell you. Some things are for pondering over and some things are for just doing without thinking, and I would hope you'd learn the difference soon enough!" Winded by her long speech, Loraine dumped a heaping teaspoon of sugar into her coffee and stirred vigorously.

Brenna cleared her throat. "I just don't want to complicate things. I told him when he got here that when he left again I didn't want to be crying by the window."

Loraine shook her head. "Child, sometimes crying by the window is better than never crying at all. You know the old saying. 'No one ever died of a broken window.'"

That wasn't quite the way the old saying went, but Brenna had learned over the years to divine the meaning of Loraine's fractured wisdom.

"By the way," Loraine said, standing up and heading toward the counter with her coffee. "Luke just drove up in your car."

Brenna's hand jerked and bumped her glass, spilling iced tea on the table. She stood and was busy mopping up the tea with her apron when the door opened and Luke walked in. Brenna looked up at him slowly, wondering if he would be able to meet her eyes after last night. Most of all she dreaded seeing the expression there. If it was cool and distant, then she didn't think she would be able to stand it.

But he was smiling at her, rocking on his heels, his thumbs hooked jauntily in his jeans pockets. He had on the black T-shirt he'd worn at the picnic, and it made his blue eyes even bluer. He had apparently showered. His black hair was damp and finger combed away from his face, except for the one dark lock that fell onto his forehead. Lord, he looked good! And the expression in his eyes as his gaze lingered on Brenna made her feel like a toddler who had to clutch the table for support.

Brenna suddenly realized she was knotting her apron in her hands, and she quickly smoothed it out.

"I've been working on your car," Luke said in a husky timbre, nodding toward the parking lot.

"And it still got you here?" Brenna asked, but her voice was teasing.

Luke grinned. "Come on. I'll show you how well it's running."

Brenna glanced at Loraine and noticed that she was unabashedly eavesdropping. "The supper crowd will be here soon," Brenna hedged.

At that, Loraine came charging around the counter like a bull after a red cape. "Now you two just shoo on out of here," she said, waving her dishrag at them. "Go on! Brenna, you've got the chicken stewing and I can make the dumplings. And Fergie'll take care of the biscuits. Now just get!"

"Don't ever run a family business," Brenna advised Luke in an undertone, smiling nevertheless as she took off her apron. She grabbed her purse from behind the counter, gave Loraine a peck on the cheek and made a hurried survey of her appearance in the mirror over the counter. She supposed she was presentable enough for a drive with Luke in her light blue skirt that buttoned down the front and matching short-sleeved cotton sweater. Her hair was tied back with a blue ribbon, and she took a second to brush back some strands from her cheek before she hurried toward the door Luke held open.

He was flexing his back and rubbing it with one palm, and Fergie chose that moment to come out of the kitchen again. "Hey, Luke!" he called. "You want me to pop your back for you? Brenna has the same trouble."

Luke groaned and Brenna felt her cheeks turning pink as they headed toward the parking lot. As the door closed Brenna could hear Loraine lecturing Fergie on the virtues of not offering his so-called medical advice unless it was asked for.

"Hey, guess where we're going!" Luke said when they were on the road, giving Brenna a light poke in the ribs.

"The heavens," she said immediately, giving in to the whimsical mood that had overtaken her.

He chuckled and gave her an appreciative look. "No, honey. Those are the *night* trips."

Brenna's skin warmed as she remembered just which night he was referring to. She looked out the window to keep him from seeing her discomfiture.

"Did I tell you yet how good you smell?" he said, and she realized he was trying to make this day-after-the-night-before easier for her.

She dared a look at him and couldn't help laughing when his eyebrows rose and lowered. "It's just stewed chicken and rhubarb pie," she said.

"Well, it's mighty fine," he assured her. "You ought to bottle it."

"Eau de Chestnut Tree Cafe," she said, realizing it wasn't so hard to relax around Luke after all. *If* she could keep her mind away from the erotic images of the two of them together last night.

"I'm going to tell you where we're going," he announced importantly. "I'm taking you to the carnival."

"I didn't know there was one here."

"Yes, indeed, and a fine carnival it is. Well, not all that fine. A Ferris wheel, a few of those rigged games and some ride that spins you around until you throw up."

Brenna laughed. "What a high recommendation."

"This is secondhand information. I heard about it from Jason Conley."

"Jason Conley?" Brenna repeated in disbelief. "Jason Conley, the farmer who must be all of sixty-five?"

"That's the one. The Conley brothers are nuts for carnivals. Can't you just picture the three of them screaming their heads off on a roller coaster?"

"No," Brenna said honestly, but the thought made her laugh.

The carnival was about twenty miles away and was just about on par with Jason Conley's description. Brenna and Luke wandered around the straw-covered grounds, stopping now and then to throw darts at balloons or pluck a plastic duck with a number from a trough. Luke put his arm around Brenna and it seemed the most natural thing in the world. It was early yet and almost no one was around, and Brenna felt herself yearning for this day to never end. With Luke there were no promises of tomorrow and Brenna was going to gather as much of today to store as she could.

"You don't want to ride that thing that makes you throw up, do you?" he asked, trying to look serious.

"Lord, no!" she said, punching his arm when she saw he was teasing her. She had always hated any ride that spun in circles or went fast.

The Ferris wheel was about her speed, and Luke bought them two tickets. From the top they could see the surrounding countryside with its neat squares of corn and soybeans and tidy white farmhouses. Here and there a tractor chugged down a field.

Brenna's stomach dipped as the Ferris wheel made its slow circuit, but she wasn't sure if it was the ride or the feel of Luke's arm around her shoulders. Luke had always transformed the ordinary into something special. Here was this little piece of magic, this carnival, in the middle of nowhere, nothing but fields and farmhouses and cattle lots as far as the eye could see.

"What are you thinking about?" he asked her softly.

"About how different things are when you're around," she said honestly, opening her eyes and looking into his face and seeing a vulnerability there that made her heart clench.

She saw the shadows leap into his eyes again, and she wished she knew what to do to banish them. "Brenna, I never meant to turn your life upside down, now or...before."

"I know that." She touched his jaw with a gentle finger, as if to see if he was a mirage. "I just wanted you to know that it's all right. Your leaving."

She meant both leavings, the one all those years ago and the one yet to come. "Brenna..." he began, his eyes clouded, but she touched his lips with her finger, silencing him.

"Don't say anything," she began. "Let's just enjoy today. Besides," she added wryly. "I don't think I could stand all the excitement if you were always here."

He smiled, but it didn't quite reach his eyes.

"Then let's not squander today," he said quietly as the Ferris wheel came to a stop. "Let's enjoy the ride as long as we can." When she looked into his face she saw such loneliness that she wanted to embrace him and cry, but he was helping her from the seat, then buying a roll of tickets.

They rode the Ferris wheel until the sky grew dark and the carnival became crowded with people. A loudspeaker piped tinny music into the dust-filled air and laughter mingled with the carny barkers' shouted invitations to try one's hand at their games. From the top of the Ferris wheel Luke and Brenna could see lights come on in farmhouse kitchens and milk barns. Reddish-brown-and-white Hereford cattle ambled toward barns in the twilight or stood alone on the hillside and lowed at the sky. The concession stands opened, and the sweet, tangy smells of popcorn and Polish sausage and funnel cakes wafted over everything.

When their tickets finally ran out, Luke and Brenna reluctantly left the Ferris wheel behind and strolled around the grounds. They stopped to buy hamburgers, then cotton candy, and leaned against a fence in a dark corner to eat. Sticky cotton candy covered Brenna's fingers and face after she finished, and Luke laughed at the mess. He pulled his handkerchief from his pocket, but then apparently had second thoughts and brought her hand to his mouth instead.

A sensual fire began at her fingertips and spread rapidly through her bloodstream as Luke put one finger at a time to his mouth and licked it clean with his tongue. His eyes captured hers and Brenna's breath came in shallow bursts. His tongue was on her palm now, and a small groan of desire escaped her. People drifted past on the main path, but no one spotted them in the shadows. Brenna was grateful for that. She couldn't keep the pleasure from her voice or her face, and she stared back into Luke's eyes with unabashed longing.

She whispered his name softly and his eyes fastened on her mouth. Slowly he pulled her to him until they were barely touching and she had to look up to see his face. In the shadows his eyes burned hot and hungry. "Sweet, sweet Brenna," he whispered before his mouth caught hers and he kissed her with a need that weakened her knees and made her curl her fingers against his chest.

As though one taste fueled the hunger for another, deeper kiss, his mouth roved over hers, plundering and leaving her robbed of all breath. Fire against fire. That was how she answered him, her mouth greedily seeking his. She could almost imagine that they were kids again, a little crazy and a lot in love.

Luke. Lord, how she'd missed him all these years. Years of a cold, lonely bed and a lonelier existence. It might be another ten years before she saw him again, and that realization brought tears to her eyes.

A young couple came running down the path, seeking the shadows themselves, and Luke slowly raised his head from Brenna's.

"How are things between us?" he whispered softly. "Did we put them right, Brenna?"

"No...yes," she said, then, "I don't know." Everything seemed right when Luke held her close like this, but when he wasn't around, some hollow ache grew inside her until nothing seemed right. Luke could tilt her whole world slightly askew until she could swear the sun was setting in the east. Damn. She'd better get used to that feeling of no Luke around, because the time would come when he would be gone again. She felt his hands caressing her shoulders, and she knew with heartbreaking certainty that she would be crying in the window when he did go.

"I want things to be okay with us," he told her, eyes searching her face. "Tell me what you need, what you want me to do."

She looked into his face, into those eyes that watched her with such intensity, and she didn't know what to tell him. Things could never be right between them because he was a racer and she was a small-town café owner. They had lost a baby and they had lost whatever tenuous threads had held them together. Nothing could fix that.

Gently she touched his face. "Those things between us, whatever they are... I've put them to rest. I can live with them now, Luke."

Liar, her heart mocked her. And Luke's blue eyes seemed to say the same thing. But he only continued to study her, until Brenna looked away. The young couple came giggling and strolling down the path again, and Luke turned and took Brenna's arm, guiding her away from the carnival and toward the car.

He held the door open for her and then leaned down when she was inside. Brenna looked at him and found herself mesmerized by his piercing gaze. "You may have put those things between us to rest, Brenna, but I haven't," he said in a husky voice. "They follow me day and night, and they have for all these years. No matter how fast the track I drove or how smooth the car, I couldn't outrun them." His eyes pinned hers a moment longer and then he swiftly closed the door and came around to the driver's side.

Brenna looked out the window to avoid his eyes, which she could feel assessing her from time to time. She felt that the admission he'd made, that he'd suffered through their

separation as much as she, was said under the spell of the
carnival and the summer night. If she tried to answer him,
then she'd end up saying things better left unsaid, things that
would tell him how very much alone she'd been and how
nothing else had salved that loneliness as much as their
lovemaking last night and this day they'd shared.

"Is that it, then?" he asked softly. She turned question-
ing eyes to him.

"You won't fight with me anymore, Brenna?"

"I thought that was one of the things that was wrong before," she said, her voice thick.

He shook his head. "No," he said. "The fighting wasn't
wrong. Fighting was just you and me thrashing things out
between us, setting them right. What was wrong was the silence." She could see the tightening of his hands on the
steering wheel and the fleeting shadows in his eyes that in-
dicated this wasn't easy for him. "Silence is the worst,
Brenna. It's the same way when a driver crashes at the track.
Inside your car you're hearing a steady whine of tires on the
track, the engines roaring, all of this muted through the
helmet. But when you go out of control, when . . . when
something happens you can't stop, then it's the silence that
overwhelms you. They say everything seems in slow motion during an accident. It is. But it's also silent. And if your
car gets airborne it's worse, because you're unconnected to
anything. You're just out there soaring through the air, no
longer in control of your own car. You can't hear the whine
anymore or engines roaring or anything. And you know that
when you do hit something—the wall or another car or the
roof of your car if you're flipping over—then the noise will
start." His eyes pierced her in the darkness a second before
they returned to the road. "That's the fear, Brenna, the
deafening silence."

Neither of them spoke. For an instant the sound of the
tires on the pavement became tires on a track and she knew
what he meant. But she had known without ever having
driven a car a hundred miles an hour. She had known all

those long, cold nights in bed when she'd waged her own battle with the silence. When she'd lain there feeling like half a person, a person whose husband and baby had been wrenched from her. Yes, the silence was deafening.

They continued without speaking the rest of the trip. They were almost at her drive when Luke downshifted and the engine died. He turned the key in the ignition, all the while guiding the car into her drive, but nothing happened. He frowned and turned the key again. Slowly the car rolled to a stop, and Luke stepped on the brake.

"What the heck—" he began.

"The solenoid," Brenna informed him, opening the door.

He poked his head out the window as she walked around behind the car and said, "How do you know that?"

"Joe told me."

"Well, why the hell didn't he put a new one in if he knew what was wrong?" Luke poked his head farther out the window. "And what are you doing behind the car?"

"I'm going to push. And Joe didn't fix the solenoid because he didn't know how." Brenna bent down and put both hands on the trunk. "Take your foot off the brake."

"No, I'm not taking my foot off the brake! You get over here this minute! What kind of brother do you have who'd let you drive a car with a bad solenoid? And how come Burgess didn't do anything about it?"

"Just leave Clinton out of this!" Brenna said, straightening as her temper got the better of her. "He's busy, too, you know."

"Yeah, busy selling cars, not fixing them," Luke shot back. "Now get over her and take the wheel while I push."

"No!"

Luke violently pulled on the emergency brake, then swung open the door and stormed over to her. "Get in the car, Brenna, or the damn thing's going to wind up in a ditch with no one steering."

"Then *you* get in the car and steer!" she insisted stubbornly, placing her hands on her hips and facing him defiantly.

"You're crazy if you think I'm going to let you push this car! Why would you want to do such a stupid thing?"

"Because you were limping a little when we left the carnival and I don't want your leg to hurt!" There. She'd said it.

He stared at her in surprise for so long that she crossed her arms and lowered her eyes, frowning.

"Brenna, honey," he said gently, "I promise you it won't hurt my leg to push this car. Now please steer it for me. You'll do that for me, won't you?"

Yes, she would, when he put it like that. She started to go around him to the open door, but a large hand closed gently around her arm. "See, honey?" he murmured with a crooked smile. "Our fights are never the problem."

A quivering feeling took over her stomach at his touch, a feeling that persisted even as he pushed the car up the drive and she steered. As they rolled up to the front of the house, the door opened and Brenna watched in astonishment as Denny stepped onto the porch. Nobody in Waldo had seen Denny for months, and even her family didn't know where he was. "Hey, Bren, where the heck have you been all evening?" he called genially, walking down the steps.

She didn't have time to answer or even to wonder what he was doing here after all this time, because apparently Luke stood at that moment and Denny saw him. Denny's face registered surprise and then chagrin.

"Now, look, Luke," Denny said defensively, backing away. "It wasn't what you think. It was all a misunderstanding."

"Yeah? And just who misunderstood the seven thousand dollars?" Luke demanded, advancing slowly on Denny.

"Well . . ." Denny didn't seem to have an answer to that, and he suddenly turned and ran, Luke right after him.

"What the heck?" Brenna wondered out loud, setting the emergency brake and jumping out to run after them.

When she rounded the side of the house Luke and Denny were rolling around on the ground, Denny apparently trying to get away and Luke trying to pin him down. "Will you hold still and listen!" Luke shouted.

"What's going on?" Brenna demanded, sidestepping as they rolled toward her.

"I covered the money!" Luke shouted, louder now. The tussle finally came to a halt, with Luke straddling Denny and glaring down at him while Denny stared back in surprise. Denny's red hair was tousled and he looked thinner than Brenna remembered.

"What's going on?" she repeated.

"Nothing," the two men said in chorus.

Luke glanced at Brenna and then slowly climbed off Denny. "Why don't you go on in the house, Brenna, so Denny and I can talk?"

Denny was standing up and brushing himself off, still keeping a wary eye on Luke.

"I'm not going anywhere," Brenna announced, "until you tell me why the two of you found it necessary to roll around the ground like a couple of acorns in a windstorm."

There was a long silence while everyone looked at everyone else in turn and then looked away. Denny finally cleared his throat. "I...got into a little trouble in Iowa a while back," he said. "I sort of got mixed up with a guy who was building race cars. Luke said not to get involved with him, but... We were supposed to be partners and we were going to build a car for this other guy, but...my, uh, partner took his half of the money and split town before we got the car built. I kind of panicked and took off with my half of the money."

"Denny!" Brenna cried. "How could you do something so stupid! I ought to whack you like you've never been whacked before!" To her irritation she saw that Luke was suddenly grinning. "And you!" She turned on Luke. "What was your part in this?"

He dug his toe into a patch of grass and tried hard to tame his grin. "I covered Denny's half of the money so he wouldn't be arrested." He spared Denny a wry glance. "Unfortunately he was so far away by then that he didn't know it."

"Yeah," Denny said abashedly. "I thought I had the sheriff and Luke both after my ass."

"Well, you should have been arrested," Brenna said angrily. "And, Luke, why on earth would you spend your own money to keep him out of jail?"

"Because he's your brother," he said shortly. "He was having problems after his divorce and he'd been drinking too much and I figured he was entitled to one mistake."

Denny grinned. "You should have seen him, Bren. He was always on my case in Iowa. Drove me home from bars lots of nights and gave me long lectures."

"Apparently they didn't sink in," she observed dryly.

"Oh, hell, yeah they did!" Denny said. "And I'm going to pay back every penny of that seven thou to Luke."

"You'd better believe you are," Brenna said grimly.

"Come on," Luke said, clapping Denny on the shoulder. "Let's go fix up a bedroom for you."

"A bedroom!" Brenna cried. "I don't remember asking him to stay!"

"Come on, Brenna," Luke coaxed her, putting his other arm around her shoulder. "You wouldn't turn away your own brother, would you? Especially after you let your ex-husband stay here."

"No kidding," Denny said. "You staying here, too, Luke?"

So then the men were off on another topic of conversation—the state of disrepair the house had fallen into, and Brenna sighed and followed them into the house. She was beginning to think that maybe finding Denny was Luke's real reason for coming back to Waldo and seeing her again was pretty far down the list.

"Hey, what's with Luke?" Denny demanded when they were upstairs in the guest bedroom and he was helping her put sheets on the bed. Luke had gone back outside to have another look at Brenna's car.

"How should I know what's with Luke?" Brenna answered peevishly.

"Well, hell, I thought you'd have a clue. I mean, he came here, didn't he?"

"His father's very sick."

"Oh, that's too bad. Lot of hard luck for him."

"What hard luck?" Brenna demanded.

"Oh, you know. The bad accident and everything. He hasn't been near a race car since then."

"What accident?" Brenna asked, trying to sound casual.

Denny glanced up at her swiftly. "He didn't say anything?" When she didn't answer, he shrugged. "I guess he had his reasons for not telling you." He remained silent after that and Brenna could have choked him for not telling her. She could have choked Luke, too. He gave her lectures about silence, then didn't tell her about something as important as a bad accident.

Damn Luke McShane anyway.

Brenna couldn't sleep that night for all her worry about Luke's return. Ostensibly, he had come back because his father was so sick, but deep inside Brenna realized she had harbored the hope that he had come back at least in part to see her. Now she was beginning to see how foolish she'd been. Of course, Luke had come to Waldo because of his father, and maybe he had come looking for Denny. At best she was a poor third on his list. She stood to go inside, feeling much like the third-place jockey in a race.

A noise arrested her on the stairs and she stopped to listen. It came from Luke's room. For a moment she thought he was talking to Denny, but then she heard Denny's even snoring from his own room. She frowned. It must be the nightmare again. Instantly she went up and stopped outside his door, where she heard him murmuring, in distress, a short, pained "Oh" again and again and then, "Oh, God, no."

She started to push open the door, her only thought to stop his pain, but the sting of coming in third in his priorities stopped her. If she went rushing to his bedside, he would know how much she cared for his well-being.

Perusing the shadows in the dark hallway, she saw the oil painting she had done of the house when they first moved in. It was American primitive at its most primitive, but Luke had always liked it and so it had stayed on the wall. The frame was solid and weighed a ton. Brenna pried it from its hook, raised it over her head and dropped it to the floor. It made a resounding crash that echoed through the house. Denny, who could sleep through a herd of elephants doing the polka, snored on.

There was a startled catch of breath from Luke, and Brenna carefully pushed open his door. He was sitting up in bed groggily, his feet tangled in the sheet, his hair tousled. Eyes heavy with sleep sought her face when she stepped inside.

"I'm sorry," she said hesitantly, quickly scanning his eyes and seeing the nightmare receding. "I was going to bed in the dark and I knocked the picture off the wall." She hoped he was too sleepy to realize she had to overshoot her room by a good ten feet to hit the picture.

"It's all right," he said in a hoarse voice. "I wasn't sleeping very well anyway." He freed his feet from the sheet and swung them to the floor, then ran a hand through his hair before standing. He was wearing only a pair of boxer shorts, and Brenna's throat went dry as her eyes drifted over his taut body. He was built for speed and control and it was no wonder he had wedded himself to a race track. But it didn't stop Brenna from wanting him. She averted her eyes, not wanting to look at what she couldn't touch.

"Brenna, are you okay?" he asked softly. "You're usually in bed by now."

"I was just going," she said, turning toward the door.

She didn't hear him move, but a gentle hand caught her shoulder and turned her to him. Don't do this to me, she begged silently. I can't stand to touch you and let you go. His bare flesh was silvery and supple in the moonlight, his chest and shoulder muscles standing out in corded relief. Strength emanated from him, not just the physical strength required to control a screaming race car careening around a track but the strength of a man who'd never broken down emotionally all the time she'd known him.

His troubled gaze traveled over her face, but it seemed powerless to tell Brenna what she needed to know. What did she mean to him? Why was he here in her house?

She couldn't stop looking at his mouth and as though her eyes had powers of their own, his lips parted slightly on a soft exhalation and he brushed his mouth against hers, softly at first and then soft exhalation and he brushed his mouth against hers, softly at first and then with an insistence that belied his weariness. "Brenna," he murmured with a groan. "I always want you so."

His words made the ache inside her grow and nearly consume her with her want and his mouth continued to take her with an insatiable hunger. "You always take the hurt away," he said, half to himself. This time his words swam inside her head, flashing there like the old film he'd run on her living room wall.

Was this what she meant to him, then? She was no more than a physical comfort after a nightmare, a warm body to hold him when his father was dying. And that hurt her, hurt her deep in her heart where a woman's pride and pain are greatest.

The hurt was so great that she pulled back and stared into his eyes. "You were in an accident, weren't you?" she said, her voice taut.

He looked momentarily surprised and his hands tightened on her shoulders. She could feel a slight trembling in them through the thin cotton. Or maybe she was the one trembling. "I... Let's not talk about that," he said. The shadows in his eyes deepened, making him suddenly seem very far away from her. "I want to hold you, Brenna. Will you let me do that?"

She wanted it, too. My God, how she wanted it! But not like this, not when she hurt so from being third best. "No," she ground out, and her own anger surprised her. She took a step away from him, and he finally let his hands fall from her shoulders. "I'm so convenient, aren't I?" she lashed out, her voice now trembling as much as his fingers had on her shoulders. "'Let me hold you, Brenna,' and then you feel all right again. What about me, Luke? What about how I feel? I hurt. I hurt damn bad! But it doesn't matter to you. What matters is that when you're feeling down, you have a pair of arms to hold you and a warm body to make love— No, not love—to have sex with!" She was damned if she would let him see her cry, and it took a great deal of effort to hold the tears in check while she stared at him furiously.

After a stunned silence, the fire leaped to his eyes. He reached for her, but when she quickly stepped backward, he dropped his hands and clenched them at his sides. "Is that what you think, that I used you?" he demanded. "That you didn't mean any more to me than a damn bed partner? We were a lot more than that together, Brenna McShane, and you're lying to both of us if you think otherwise."

"And you didn't lie to both of us, Luke?" she demanded in a deadly voice, hearing herself pushing things too far but unable to stop. "You didn't lie when you said those marriage vows and then left the minute things got tough? You never hung around long enough to be anything other than a damn bed partner!" She was sorry she'd said the words the instant they were out. She didn't even mean them, but it was too late.

His face drained of color and she opened her mouth, stricken, trying to think of something to assuage the pain she'd just inflicted. "Luke—"

But he brushed away her attempt with a wave of his hand. "Go on back to bed, Brenna," he said harshly. "Surely an empty bed is better than one with me in it."

He was turning around, his body rigid, and she knew he wouldn't tolerate her touch or her words now. Slowly, with infinite misery, she backed out of the room and walked barefoot to her own bed.

Dear God, she asked herself, what have I done? Why had she said such awful things? It wasn't until an hour later, when she was still staring at the ceiling through a watery haze of tears, that she realized she'd said them because she wanted him to leave now before it hurt any more. She wanted him gone because she still loved him.

Seven

———

The blue-plate special is Tuna Noodle Bake with peas, not *pita pockets*!'' Brenna announced in irritation as she vigorously sponged off the blackboard sitting on the counter. ''I didn't buy all those cans of tuna to have them sit around here with nobody eating them!''

''People will *love* pita pockets!'' Fergie countered, reaching out to try to wrestle the chalk from her.

''Stop that!'' Brenna ordered him. ''No pita pockets.''

Fergie sighed in apparent defeat. ''You got to educate folks' tastebuds around here, Brenna. Give 'em a sample of French cooking and stuff now and then.'' Brenna went on writing Tuna Noodle Bake on the blackboard, and Fergie sighed. ''And speaking of eatin', seems to me something's been eating at you for a couple of days now.''

Brenna dropped the chalk, frowned and picked it up again. This time it broke when she tried to write. She pitched it on the counter in disgust and banged open the door to the kitchen. Damn! Something was eating her all right, and it had been slowly gnawing away inside her in the two days since the confrontation in Luke's bedroom. It was the growing realization of just how much she loved Luke McShane and just how futile that love was. She had carefully avoided Luke since that night, and where he ate his meals or when he slept was unknown to her. Denny, of course, insisted on joining Brenna for breakfast, lunch and dinner. She was so unnerved by his constant commentary on the state of siege between her and Luke that she had almost dumped his spaghetti over his head the night before. Sighing, she snatched the bottle of antacid from the shelf by the spices and dumped two onto her palm.

"Pita pockets," she muttered to herself, chewing rapidly.

"Heads up in the kitchen!" Fergie sang out as he pushed open the swinging door. "Visitor coming through!"

"Fergie, this kitchen is not a stop on the Waldo grand tour," Brenna said, but her irritation fizzled out when she looked up and saw Luke right behind Fergie.

Luke's eyes met hers, then quickly slid away. "I've got your dad and Joe and Denny outside in your dad's truck," he said hesitantly.

"What did you do, hog-tie them all together?" she asked dryly. Despite her resolve, her gaze traveled over his clean jeans and white T-shirt and on up to the face studying her gravely. His black hair shone in the overhead light, and Brenna desperately wanted to reach out the brush back the lock falling across his forehead.

Fergie kept popping up behind Luke's shoulders, first one side, then the other, darting curious glances at Brenna and obviously trying to assess the situation.

"Will you please stop hovering?" Brenna finally demanded testily, and he gathered his wounded dignity and marched out the door to the counter area. "What are you doing here?" Brenna asked Luke.

"That's the eternal question with you, isn't it?" he said wryly, then shrugged apologetically. "I thought you might like to know that I'm now gainfully employed. Denny and I got jobs with Avery at Custom Rebuilding.''

Brenna chewed her lip. "For how long?"

Briefly the shadows chased across his eyes and then cleared. "Are you that anxious for me to be gone?" he asked.

Brenna shrugged and looked away from him, pretending to scrutinize the row of pots hanging over the sink. "I just don't picture you sticking with it very long."

There was a silence while she felt Luke's eyes on her. "I don't think you're worried about when I'll *get tired* of things around here and leave," he said quietly. "I think you're thinking I might be planning to stick around. And for some reason that scares the hell out of you, Brenna." She glanced at him as he jammed his hand in his pocket and pulled out his keys. His eyes connected with hers and locked, and at that moment Brenna saw the truth in what he'd said. "We're driving over to Springfield to pick up some door handles for your dad," he said. "It might be late when we get back." He turned his back on her and left, and Brenna realized that she'd been holding her breath tightly in her chest.

Luke had said late, but 1:00 a.m. qualified as more than just late. Brenna checked the clock for the hundredth time and picked up the photo album in her lap. She hadn't showered or changed into her nightgown yet, afraid that if Luke had car trouble she might miss the phone call. But then, why would he call her anyway? They'd done nothing but fight lately.

She curled her legs under her on the couch and tried to focus on the pictures instead. But Luke's words kept coming back to haunt her. *You're thinking I might be planning to stick around.* No! She wouldn't let herself believe that for a minute. Luke might stick around for a short while, but before long he would tire of Avery's job and pine for the racing circuit. She'd been through that too often to delude herself into imagining Luke could ever put down roots.

Some men were born to be footloose, and Luke Mc-Shane was of that breed.

And yet . . . The ache inside her grew as she looked at the pictures of the two of them together during their brief married life. These pictures weren't like the movies. These pictures were slices of time, frozen forever, and she could study them. What she saw on Luke's face surprised her. Why hadn't she noticed that grin of delight before? Had he really been that enthusiastic over a silly picnic in the middle of their new apple orchard the day they'd planted the trees? And he looked genuinely engrossed in painting their name on the mailbox, as though it meant something.

Brenna brushed her palms over her eyes as tears burned. Fools that they were, they had once had something very special and they'd let it get away. She supposed she was afraid that if Luke stayed, she would grieve forever for what had once been.

She jumped when the phone rang, dropping the album on the floor. My God, what if he'd been in an accident? She ran to the kitchen in her bare feet and jerked the phone from its hook.

"Brenna? It's me, Luke."

"What's wrong? What happened?"

"Now, nothing's wrong. Well, I mean it's nothing to worry about. Everybody's okay."

"For God's sake, McShane! What happened? Where are you?"

"At the county jail."

"You're in jail?! What on earth did you do now?" Brenna closed her eyes and pictured her hands closing on his neck.

"I said we're *at* the county jail, not *in* it. There's a difference, you know. There was this little altercation at the tavern where we stopped for a hamburger on the way home. Denny said hello to some girl and it turned out her boyfriend was just coming back from the john and misunderstood and he'd had a beer or two too many and...well, you know how it is.''

"No, I don't know how it is," she said pointedly.

Luke cleared his throat. "Well, the thing is the guy had a buddy and they ganged up on Denny, and your dad and Joe and me...well, listen, Bren, have you got two hundred dollars around the house?''

"Two hundred dollars!''

"Now don't go getting upset, Bren. You see, the sheriff wasn't going to make your dad and Joe and me post bail, seeing as how we've never been in trouble and all, but the other guys in the fight started screaming about the sheriff going easy on us and everything... Listen, Bren, do you think you could just bring the money?''

In the end she had to go by Loraine's house, and between their cookie jars they had the two hundred dollars. Loraine wanted to go with her, but with Brenna muttering about how she should "leave them all to rot in the slammer,'' Loraine apparently had second thoughts and stayed home. It was thirty miles to the county seat, and the drive was not conducive to alleviating Brenna's bad mood. She posted the bond at the front desk, then told the clerk she would be waiting in the car.

Joe, Denny, Robert and Luke came strolling down the courthouse steps, poking each other in the ribs and laughing, and Brenna tightened her grip on the steering wheel. It was dark, but they got the picture as soon as Joe opened the door on the passenger side. "You," Brenna ordered crisply. "In front. The rest of you can sit in back.''

"But, honey," her dad pleaded. "There's not a lot of room back there. Couldn't you let Luke drive and you sit in the back?''

"No, Daddy, that's not possible," Brenna said coolly. "I'm assuming you'll find the back seat more comfortable than a jail cell.'' That apparently settled the issue because they all quieted down and meekly took their assigned seats. The silence lengthened on the trip back home, and there were whispers of "good night" and "wasn't it a good fight" when she dropped her dad and Joe at Loraine's house.

"I'll go get the pickup tomorrow," Robert said, poking his head in the back window.

"We ran over a broken bottle in the parking lot and got two flat tires," Denny explained to Brenna, and then, noticing the expression on her face, he settled down into silence again.

At the house Brenna hopped out, slammed the door and headed for the front porch before Denny and Luke had a chance to move. By the time she heard them come inside she was already in the shower.

The hot water relaxed her some, and she pulled on her newest nightgown, the one that had whetted such curiosity in Luke and Loraine and Fergie. It was floor-length and more lace than rose-colored fabric. The straps were wisps of lace, and when Brenna surveyed herself in the mirror she saw that she looked ready for more than sleeping. Frowning, she tugged on a short, terry robe that matched the sheer gown about as well as . . . as pita pockets matched her customers' appetites.

She could hear Denny snoring already when she stepped into the hall, but Luke's door was half open and the little light on the night table was on. He was wearing only jeans, and Brenna stood mesmerized by the sight of his arm and chest muscles moving fluidly in the soft light. He was sitting sideways to her, his bare right foot resting on the floor, his left leg bent on the bed as he sewed his shirt. Absorbed in his task, he didn't hear her move closer to his door.

He turned briefly toward the light, his eyes still intent on the shirt, and Brenna's mouth opened soundlessly. An angry-looking cut on his left cheekbone was red and swollen and he looked so tired.

It was impossible for her to go on to bed knowing he was hurt, so she pushed his door open the rest of the way and said brusquely, "Here, let me do that."

He looked up, surprised, but handed her the shirt. Brenna sat on the end of the bed, facing him, and clucked over the tear. "You should have taken home ec in high school. This looks like it was stitched with a jackhammer. Where did you get the needle and thread anyway?"

"Bottom right drawer by the sink. You always kept your sewing kit there."

She glanced up, surprised that he'd remembered, and saw him looking at her attire curiously. "That's an *interesting-looking* nightgown you're wearing." He cleared his throat, and she almost smiled, watching him try to get a better look. "That robe doesn't do much for it though."

Carefully she laid the shirt on the trunk at the end of the bed. "I'd better put a patch on that tomorrow," she said. "It's a big tear."

"Brenna—"

She jumped up before he could say anything. "You've got a nasty cut. I'll get something for it."

When she came back and sat on the bed, he obediently turned his face for her and she dabbed at the cut with a piece of gauze soaked in antiseptic.

"Ow!" he complained. "What's that?"

"Hold still. I've got to clean this. You don't want an infection." Her bare arm kept brushing his bare chest, and her fingers were trembling as she worked. She sat back to let the liquid dry and his eyes met hers.

"I'm sorry about tonight," he said quietly.

Brenna shrugged, her anger dissipated. "Denny was always getting into something like that. I shouldn't have gotten so mad at all of you."

"He's doing better, Brenna. It may not seem that way, but he's changed."

"Changed?" she repeated wryly. "Once he hit puberty he was never around long enough for me to get to know who he was. I didn't know the original Denny, much less this changed one. How much trouble was he in, Luke?"

Luke was silent a moment. "He took his divorce hard. He always overdid things and it got worse. He drank more, got in more fights, fell in with the wrong crowd. I'd see him now and then, and this year I talked him into going to that little support group I told you about, the one I started." Luke stared down at his hands on his lap, turning one palm up and absently rubbing it with his other hand. "He was doing a lot better and then he got mixed up with that so-called car builder. He was in a little trouble over that."

Brenna had a feeling that Denny had been in a lot of trouble over that and Luke had done more for Denny than pay off the missing money.

"Thank you for helping him, Luke," Brenna said, idly plucking at the bedspread. "It means . . . a lot to me."

"Brenna," he said softly. When she didn't look at him, a gentle hand turned her face up. "Brenna, I didn't do it as a favor or because . . ."

His voice trailed off, leaving her to wonder what he had meant to say. Why had he been so kind to Denny and to her father and Joe? It was Luke's way to help someone out, but after the divorce he would have had good reason to put her family out of his mind once and for all.

"Why, Luke?" she whispered.

This time his gaze slid away and his hand dropped. "I didn't want to think of you going through any more pain, because of me or Denny or anyone."

Her throat ached with tears she hastily bit back. She cared about his pain, too, but had been able to do nothing to ease it for him.

"I couldn't help you when we . . . when we lost Dory," he said, his voice taut. The shadows gathered in his eyes again, and weariness and misery etched themselves in the lines around them. "I wanted to so badly, but I couldn't help you or myself. I've carried that failure with me all these years, Brenna, and it's been tearing me up."

"Don't, Luke," she groaned, her hands reaching out to cup his face, the face she loved so much. The coarse stubble on his jaw was rough against her palms, but she welcomed the feeling. It had been so long since she had let herself really feel either pain or pleasure. "I couldn't help us, either."

She sought his eyes to see what was there, and her heart broke when she saw why he had those cold shadows. Behind them was all the pain and loneliness she felt, as well. Tears blurred her vision and her hands touched his body blindly, trying to find the comfort they both needed so badly.

He groaned her name and pulled her to him, cradling her against his chest. She reached up one hand to cup his face and her palm grazed the moisture on his cheek. "Dear Luke," she whispered brokenly. "My phantom husband."

He laid his face against her hair, and she could feel his uneven breathing as he struggled with his emotions. Hard, callused hands held her pressed tightly against him, hands that caressed her with the comfort she sought.

"I need you, Brenna," he whispered raggedly. "I've always needed you."

"God help me, I need you, too," she answered in return, her fingers stroking his face and jaw and throat. He was such a beautiful man, she marveled, with muscles crafted for guiding a streaking car or touching a woman in pleasure. She loved him so much, and she would take the heartbreak of his leaving as long as she could have one more night with Luke McShane.

She tilted up her face and Luke's mouth took hers hungrily. His hands impatiently pulled the short terry robe from her shoulders and tossed it on the floor. The light in Luke's eyes was brighter and yet gentler than the light from the lamp. His mouth came back to hers again and tasted, and he groaned aloud. His hands touched her everywhere, caressing, making her tremble with her arousal.

"Look at you," he murmured, his hands on her shoulders, thumbs circling her collar bones. "Look how beautiful you are."

Brenna gave him a tremulous smile. Because he found her beautiful, she found it easy to be so. "And the night-gown?" she teased him softly. "Is it beautiful, too?"

"Oh, my, yes," he agreed, his eyes filling with desire.

"Well, now you know what was in that Penney's bag," she told him. "It's silly, isn't it? I buy these things for my-self all the time, and you're the first person to see me in one. I've been the best-dressed celibate in Waldo for years."

"Don't say that," he whispered, hands stroking down her arms and to her hips. There was a smile on his lips, but he was serious. "You're a woman, a very desirable woman, and you shouldn't ever deny yourself the things that go with that."

His head came forward slowly, and he nibbled enticingly on her neck, making her squirm in pleasure. After laying her back on the bed, Luke leaned on one elbow, letting his eyes take his pleasure in her before his hands and mouth fol-lowed suit.

He slid the straps down her shoulders, baring her breasts, and he began to kiss and caress them with his tongue. He made gentle swirling patterns and then sucked, making her reach for his shoulders and tighten her fingers on them. She had never known another lover, had never wanted to, be-cause Luke knew her body intimately, seemed to know her every desire. He touched her in every sensitive place that cried out for his ministrations, nibbled and licked and drove her nearly mad with pleasure.

He gently brought her up to him with his hands on her shoulders and, cradling her against him, pulled the night-gown to her waist. "Stand up, love," he whispered. She did and the gown slid to the floor. Luke's eyes roved over her appreciatively and he reached out slowly to touch her with a trembling caress.

Brenna felt her knees weakening and she sat down on the bed again. Luke's hands stroked her breasts, then her hips and then her thighs, parting them until she lay down with a ragged sigh. First he pleasured her with fingers and then with his mouth, and Brenna nearly cried with the force of the desire rippling through her.

His fingers hovered at her lips and traced their shape. His tongue followed as Brenna arched her back and strained toward him. Pulling him to her, Brenna reveled in the feel of the steely planes and sinews of his back and sides. Her fingers traced the body she remembered so well, her fingernails skimming his flat stomach and making him suck in his breath abruptly as they teased below the waistband of his jeans.

Luke stood and undressed quickly. Then he was kneeling between her legs, his hands stroking her breasts again, trailing lower, making every inch of her flesh quiver with a gnawing hunger for him.

So slowly that it seemed an eternity, Luke entered her, and still her hunger grew. He moved and then stopped, and Brenna's restless eyes focused on his face. It was suffused with a need that took her breath away. He reached down to cradle her waist and then he lifted her up so that her breasts brushed his chest and her mouth was only inches from his.

"Tonight, in this bed," he said hoarsely and evenly, "this is the last ten years. This is how much I've wanted you those years, how I've thought of you every night, of the millions of times I've said your name alone in the dark. This is what we always had between us, Brenna, and it's more."

He began moving slowly, and Brenna arched her back, her hair drifting off her shoulders and cascading behind her in a red-gold curtain. This was ten years of desire, of wanting and aching and crying in the dark. She had called his name, too, though most often in twilight sleep when her phantom lover invaded her dreams. And now that she was in his arms those ten years came rushing back in this one act.

We never really left each other, Luke thought as he felt the pleasure consume his body. He held back, forced himself to go slowly because he wanted so much to give Brenna this same pleasure, to hear her say his name in passion, a sound

as sweet to him as the wind in the trees at this old house he'd
once shared with her.

Her beautiful hair glimmered in the lamplight and he let
his fingertips stretch up to touch it. Her eyes were half
closed but they never wavered from his face, and he saw the
desire and the fever in their brown depths. Her lips were
parted and a soft breath escaped them each time he thrust.
Her skin was so pale and soft that he wanted to spend an
eternity making love to her. He wanted this to go on forever, but even now he felt his control slipping.

He could handle snarling steel at breathtaking speeds, but
this woman was his undoing. His breath rasped from his
chest, and Brenna dug her nails into his back as she made a
soundless cry. *Oh, sweet, you don't know what you're doing
to me.* His breath caught in his throat and he hung sus-
pended a second, like a hawk riding an air current. Then his
body shuddered and fell away into a dark, sweet, nameless
place. She was his again, he thought fleetingly as he went
over the edge, hearing his name escape her lips in a ragged
cry.

Brenna awoke to a sound that went straight to her heart
like a knife. Luke was groaning in his sleep again. Brenna
opened her eyes immediately and found herself in his embrace, his arm flung over her in sleep. His fingers were
clenching and unclenching on the sheet draped over her
waist and Brenna felt helpless in the face of his nightmare.
Slowly she slid out from under his arm and grabbed her
robe, pausing to look back at the bed.

It was early yet, but the room was beginning to lighten
and she could see Luke's features clearly. His mouth opened
slightly with each wrenching sound; his body was rigid as
honed muscles strained against some demon she didn't
know. Afraid to waken him and face the rejection she'd
suffered before when she confronted him about the nightmare, Brenna hurriedly slipped out of the room.

She was dressed and frying eggs when Luke entered the kitchen. Their eyes met and he stopped beside her, leaning over to lift her hair and brush his lips across the nape of her neck. "You're really something, you know that?" he whispered, and she offered him a tentative smile.

"How did you sleep?" she asked, wanting him to let the last barrier fall between them. Talk to me about it, she begged silently.

"All right," he said noncommittally, and Brenna's heart clenched in misery. There was still this between them.

At the sound of Denny's steps on the stairs, Luke moved away and began pouring coffee.

"I've got to get Dad's old shotgun and send that lousy mockingbird back to his maker," Denny complained as he padded into the kitchen on bare feet, socks and sneakers in one hand. "That damn thing woke me up at the crack of dawn. Hell, it was more like the middle of the night."

Brenna couldn't help smiling a little at that. Denny had always been the late sleeper in the family, and there had been more than one mockingbird to disrupt his sleep when they were children. It was the one thing that could wake him up.

"Don't you harm a feather on his head," she warned him. "He makes a great alarm clock."

"Yeah, well I bet Luke couldn't get any sleep, either, because of him."

Brenna looked around at Luke and found him watching her, a teasing smile on his face. "I slept real well, Denny," Luke said, still looking at Brenna. "Not long, but well."

Denny glanced at one and then the other and shook his head. "Well, it beats me how the two of you can get a good night's sleep what with crickets and mockingbirds and katydids screaming outside while it's still dark."

Brenna grinned at that and went back to fixing breakfast.

Brenna arrived at the café as the sun was cresting the adjacent field, and she found Loraine already inside arguing with Fergie over their perpetual bone of contention—bran muffins.

Brenna refereed, deciding that the muffins could remain on the menu, but five dozen was a tad too many to bake for their crowd. She mixed the pancake batter, checked on the egg delivery and popped some blueberry muffins in the oven, then went out front to inspect the counters.

The bell over the door heralded the arrival of their first customers, the Conley brothers, who headed for their usual booth in the back. Loraine stopped polishing the napkin holders and got the coffeepot. The bell tinkled again. Brenna looked up to see Clinton Burgess walking in, wearing his three-piece summer suit and a grim expression on his face. He came straight to the counter and sat in front of Brenna.

"Good morning, Clinton," she said, taking a pot of decaffeinated coffee and pouring him a cup. "How are you doing today?"

"I'm sure I'm doing better than you are, Brenna," he said. "I told you having Luke around would come to no good."

"What in heaven's name are you talking about, Clinton?" Brenna frowned and set the coffeepot on the counter.

"Last night. I heard about that ruckus at the tavern. This time Luke ended up getting your whole family arrested. Brenna, what are people going to think?"

Loraine chose that moment to walk behind Brenna and throw out her own personal observation. "*I* wasn't arrested," she said with a sniff.

Brenna sighed. "Clinton, what happened was not Luke's fault. And as for what people think, I wouldn't give one of Fergie's bran muffins for anybody's opinion, anyway."

"That's the problem, Brenna," Clinton continued in his earnest critique of her life. "You haven't cared at all what people thought ever since Luke got here. You're seen places with him, you bail him out of jail, you're still letting him stay at your house. Brenna, this isn't like you.''

"Clinton, maybe it's more like me than you know.''

He shook his head emphatically. "This is like you were when you married McShane. You didn't care about anybody's opinion then, either. And look where it got you. He'll take off again this time, Brenna. I'm telling you, you can't trust a man like that.''

Brenna tried to keep her voice calm. "Clinton, maybe it's high time I started not caring about what people think. Waldo isn't exactly the social-etiquette capital of the world, and I can't believe it's of any great importance to anyone else what Luke and I do.''

"Brenna, can't you see what's happening?'' Clinton stood in his agitation, nearly spilling his coffee. "You're wasting your potential again.''

Brenna's patience came to an end. "Oh, hell, Clinton! Wasting potential! What kind of nonsense is that? If I've wasted my so-called potential it's been the last ten years when I gave up on life.''

But Clinton went on as if he hadn't heard her. "You take up with a man like Luke McShane again despite all the heartache he gave you in the past! Sometimes you don't make sense, Brenna. Sometimes you do things that make me wonder why I still bother worrying about you.''

"Oh?'' Brenna said angrily. "And what things are those, Clinton?''

He gave a frustrated shrug of his shoulders. "Like all the time you spend with those kids. I thought at first it was because you lost your baby and this was some kind of temporary substitute. But you're still doing it, Brenna, after all these years. Hell, those kids will never grow up. They'll never amount to anything, and McShane'll never amount to anything. You're just wasting your time!''

"That's the trouble with you, Clinton,'' Brenna said in cold fury. "If a human being isn't a potential car buyer, then they aren't worth two seconds of your time.''

"That's not fair!" he cried. He reached into his pocket and threw three quarters down on the counter. "I can see I'm wasting my time," he said in an offended tone.

"And we all know how you hate to waste anything," Brenna said dryly.

"Goodbye, Brenna. I just hope you don't come crying to me when this doesn't work out."

The door banged and Brenna stared at it with a mixture of anger and sadness. Once Clinton had been her good friend, but somewhere they had grown far apart and she mourned the loss.

Loraine breezed past her to refill the coffeepot. "Well, if that wasn't a great way to start the day," she muttered. "That boy's in dire need of a decent breakfast to take an edge off his surliness."

"It's not his fault," Brenna said, still sad about losing his friendship.

"So when have you started making excuses for Clinton Burgess? Or is it Luke McShane who's put that expression on your face?"

"What expression?" Brenna demanded, trying to rearrange her facial features.

"That expression right there where your lips pucker and your brows turn down in the middle and you look like a schoolmarm about to deliver a lecture. Is that Clinton's doing or Luke's?"

"Mostly Luke's," Brenna admitted, giving up the battle.

"You and that boy sure do rile each other up," Loraine noted admiringly, "What's he gone and done now?"

"Nothing, really," Brenna said. "It's just that...well, he won't talk to me. There are things between us, things he won't tell me about, and I'm afraid it's going to be just like before. He's been having nightmares, Loraine, and Denny let it slip that Luke was in a bad accident, but when I asked him about it, he wouldn't tell me."

"Maybe he needs the right time, honey," Loraine said slowly, wiping the counter. "Men are like that sometimes.

They can't just blurt things out the way women do.'' Loraine cocked her head to inspect Brenna. ''You're making this sound awfully one-sided. Have you told him about his college money?''

Brenna shook her head. ''That's different.'' When Denny had told her that Luke was going back to school to get a degree, Brenna had given him money for Luke's tuition but made him tell Luke the money was his. What she didn't need was Luke McShane thinking he was indebted to her for anything.

''Oh, Lordy! If that ain't the battle cry between the sexes! 'That's different.' Brenna honey, there's talk and then there's talk, and it seems to me you two aren't doing much of the right kind.''

''No, I guess we aren't.'' Brenna poured herself a cup of coffee.

''And in the meantime you just goin' to mope around with the miseries?''

The door to the kitchen banged open and Fergie breezed through, carrying a tray of bran muffins with green polka dots. ''What do you think of these?'' he demanded with pride. ''Put some gooseberries in 'em.''

''Speaking of the miseries...'' Brenna said, rolling her eyes.

''Now what's *that* supposed to mean?'' Fergie demanded.

So Brenna set about restoring Fergie's good humor, all the while wondering why she was having no luck straightening out things between her and Luke.

Eight

Luke's father was worse. It was two days since Luke and Brenna had made love in Luke's bedroom, building a tentative bridge of sorts between the two of them and their raw emotions. Brenna had asked to come to the hospital with Luke, seeing the toll the visits took on him. Now, driving home from the hospital and seeing Luke with such a lost, tired expression on his face, she wasn't sure she should have come.

They were passing the high school, and Luke slowed the car. "Do you mind if we stop a minute?" he asked. Brenna shook her head.

It was a cool, clear night, the kind where the stars hung so low you could almost touch them. Luke walked with his hands in his jeans pockets, his head tilted down, and Brenna trailed along beside him, hugging her bare arms and staring out across the football field. They came to the bleachers and Luke sat in the second row, stretching out his legs on the seat in front of him.

He reached out a hand to Brenna and helped her step across the first row to sit beside him. The field was silent except for the chirping chorus of young frogs and the distant whine of a car engine on the highway.

The chill air was raising gooseflesh on Brenna's bare arms and she curled her fingers around them for warmth. "Come here," Luke said quietly. "You're cold." He tugged her against him, wrapping his left arm around her, and she absorbed the warmth from his body, her head against his shoulder.

They sat that way a long while, and Brenna remembered the times she'd sat on these very bleachers holding her breath as Luke caught the football high over his head and then ran down the field, pursued by the opposing team. Sometimes one of them caught up to him and threw him to the ground, and then Brenna would hold her breath until he got up again, wondering how hurt he was. It seemed they'd both been thrown to the ground a lot since then, but somehow they were on their feet and here together again.

"I was racing one Sunday in Iowa," Luke began quietly. "It was a night a lot like this, cool and clear. Bugs swarmed around the track lights, and I could feel adrenaline pumping the minute I put on my helmet." Brenna could feel his heartbeat beneath her cheek, strong and sure and even, and she touched the fingers of her right hand to his fingers resting on her arm, because she wanted him to go on. For once she wanted to hear about the track, to understand what it was that drew him there.

"It was a fast track," he said. "When we started the engines I could feel my blood pounding in my arms in anticipation, like always. It's a feeling…like I can fly. Like I can reach out and touch the sky. That's what the track does to me, Brenna. It makes me feel high, like everything is coming together for me." His fingers twined themselves with hers. "The only other time I get that feeling is when I'm making love to you, when I'm deep inside you and you're so soft and warm, and then the whole world's mine." Gently he brushed his jaw across her hair and she felt a trembling in his body.

"It's like that for me, too," she whispered. "Nothing else matters then."

"Nothing," he agreed. "This night I had the same feeling in the car. I was third coming around the first turn, and I hung there for a while following the leader and the second-place guy, Mike, a good friend of mind. I made my move after the fifth lap, and Mike did, too. We passed the leader and went into the turn neck and neck. If I'd glanced over I could have seen him, and I know he would have been grinning. He loved racing as much as I did. But I kept my eyes on the track and the turn, and my whole body was leaning into it. I felt like a bird gliding over a canyon, and the track noises seemed to fade." His fingers tightened on hers as though holding on to some lifeline. "Then our rear wheels touched. It wasn't anybody's fault, just some stupid accident, but it sent us both flying apart from each other. I went into a spin and I tried to ride it out, but somebody was coming up on me from behind, and he couldn't avoid me. I felt this tremendous force, like a huge shove, and then I was up in the air. The car was sailing through the air like a toy airplane in a wind. Everything slowed down and got silent, and it seemed like an eternity. Then the force hit me from the front and at the same time this awful noise erupted, like metal crashing down around your head and banging and banging and banging. And I felt like my whole body was in a vise, being squeezed so tight."

Brenna swallowed around the lump in her throat and she could feel Luke's heartbeat racing as fast as her own. "That was what I was always so afraid of," she whispered shakily. "I dreaded hearing the phone ring late at night when you were off at the track."

"I know," he murmured. "I know how hard I made it for you." He sighed and it was almost a groan. "The phone rang for someone else that night. I had a bad broken leg and a concussion, but Mike was dead. His wife was usually at the track, but that night she had the flu so she was home. He was a good friend, Brenna, a real good friend.''

"I'm sorry, Luke.'' She was sorry for more than Mike's death. She was sorry for all those nights she hadn't been there with Luke when he was racing. Maybe it would have made some difference in their marriage.

"I still dream about the crash. I try to steer away before our wheels touch, but it just goes on happening over and over. I didn't want...I didn't mean to tell you all that. I've never talked about it with anyone else.''

"I wanted you to tell me,'' she said fiercely, her free hand reaching up to touch his face. "I needed to have you tell me.''

She could feel him slowly shake his head. "It was just one more grief to lay at your feet, one more burden I've given you.''

"No!'' she said emphatically. "No, Luke. It's not that. What happened between us—those griefs—they're not just yours. Don't you see? They're part of both of us. It's so hard when you're not here, when I know you're off alone somewhere—'' She broke off and Luke gathered her into his arms and just held her for a long time, until both their heartbeats slowed and the night sounds of the field settled around them again.

"I haven't even been to a track since the accident,'' he said at last, and she heard the pain in his voice. He hesitated. "I need to go to Iowa again...to the track where it happened. I want you to go with me next weekend, Brenna.''

She could feel the tension in his body as he held her, and she knew that he was seeking something. Like Brenna, he was haltingly trying to overcome their past, their brief marriage when she would wait at home, alone and in the dark, while he was racing.

"All right,'' she said softly. "I'll go.''

"Thank you, Brenna,'' he whispered, and she felt the tension leave his arms.

They were both stiff from sitting in one position so long, and when they stood, Luke groaned. "It's hell getting old," he muttered.

"Speak for yourself," she retorted tartly. He swatted her on the behind, chasing her all the way to the car.

They joined the sprinkling of cars at the Dairy Delight on the way home, Luke claiming he couldn't go more than a week without an Elvis Burger. The first neon *D* had burned out, and the spring on the screen door was so rusted that it had lost all resiliency so that they had to squeeze through a twelve-inch opening to get inside.

Denny was sitting at the counter, nursing a shake. Luke dropped onto the stool next to him, motioning Brenna to the stool at his right. "So, how you doing?" he asked Denny.

"Not so hot," Denny said without looking at him. "I ran into Judy tonight at the store." Judy was Denny's ex-wife. She'd remarried in the last year, causing Denny no end of grief.

"Yeah? Well, at least you're drowning your sorrows in a milkshake instead of a beer. That's something anyway."

Denny shrugged, his shoulders slumped, and Luke slowly rubbed his jaw. He turned around on the stool and studied the cars in the parking lot, then pulled a ten-dollar bill from his pocket. "Give us a couple of Elvis Burgers and four chocolate shakes, would you, Marvin?" he said to the laconic young boy behind the counter. "Denny, you come with me."

Denny had no time to protest as Luke grasped his shirt sleeve and hauled him toward the door. Brenna watched in confusion. "What are you doing?" she demanded in tandem with Denny, but Luke didn't answer. Not wanting to be left behind in all this, Brenna followed them into the parking lot.

Luke was craning his head down to look into car windows, Denny sputtering protests as he was dragged in his wake. "Geez, Luke! What the hell are you doing?"

Luke stopped triumphantly and rapped his knuckles on the roof of a car. "Julie!" he called. "Hey!"

A blond head poked out the window and Brenna recognized the nurse from the hospital. She looked momentarily startled, then apparently realized that it was Luke McShane who was rapping his knuckles on her car's roof and that this was the kind of behavior one expected from him. "Luke! What is it?"

"Julie, I want you to meet someone." Luke unceremoniously dragged Denny forward and made the introductions. "Julie, this is Brenna's brother Denny. Denny, say hello to Julie."

Denny shifted from one foot to the other in acute embarrassment, gritting his teeth as he nodded to Julie and mumbled a hello. By now, heads were popping out of cars all around them. Even Marvin had come to the door to observe.

"He's a bit shy," Luke explained to Julie. "What he was wondering is if you'd go to the races in Iowa next Sunday night with him. He'd be thrilled."

Denny opened his mouth and stared at Luke in wordless panic. Luke nudged him in the ribs with an elbow.

"He doesn't look thrilled," Julie noted doubtfully.

"Take my word for it," Luke assured her. "Right, Denny?"

Denny swallowed and nodded. "Sure."

Julie smiled at Denny. "Okay. Sounds like fun to me."

"There, you see?" Luke said, thumping Denny's back. "That was easy, wasn't it? Come on inside, Julie, and have a milkshake with us."

"Luuuuke," Denny was whispering from between clenched teeth, but Luke was not to be deterred as he helped Julie from her car.

Julie winked at Brenna as she met her at the door. "Your Luke's not an easy man to say no to, is he?"

"He's a one-man whirlwind," Brenna agreed dryly, watching Luke busy himself seating Denny and Julie next to each other like a fussy matchmaker.

"There!" he said, sitting beside Brenna with a wide grin. "How about that?"

"How about that?" she echoed, smiling in spite of herself. Luke's face was a study in self-satisfaction. "Luke McShane, do you have to *fix* everything you run across?" she asked, half in exasperation, half in amusement.

"Pretty much so," he admitted, the grin widening.

Brenna laughed and caught herself meeting his eyes and feeling that uncontrollable longing in her belly. Oh, Lord, she thought with an ache of despair. He's still the same Luke McShane, and I still can't help loving him.

Saturday was hot, and Brenna closed the café herself at eight that night after sending Fergie and Loraine on home. Her house was empty and humid when she got there, and she opened all the windows to air it out.

She poured herself a glass of iced tea and went to sit on the top step of the front porch where a slight breeze stirred. She barely touched the tea, though, letting it sit on the wooden boards until the ice melted and the glass was wet with condensation.

Fireflies winked as dusk fell, heat lightning glowed on and off in the western sky like a hot, empty promise. Luke's car turned into her drive and Brenna watched it kick up a cloud of dust.

It was a summer night like those she remembered from so long ago with Luke driving in after dark, and yet it was different. Then she had despaired of ever having Luke Mc-Shane all to herself. She knew how much he belonged to racing and cars. But now she found herself ten years older and a lot less wiser as her heart persisted in entertaining thoughts of Luke McShane staying here with her. He was her chimera, her mythical beast. She knew with every brain cell she still possessed that he could never be content with just Waldo, but some small piece of her carried the dream that he could be tamed, that he could learn contentment.

He stopped for a moment when he saw her sitting on the porch in the dark, and then he walked slowly up the steps and sat down beside her. He lifted the glass of tea questioningly and she nodded. Luke drank deeply, and Brenna's eyes roved over him restlessly.

He'd been working long, hard hours at Avery's, and it showed. His dark hair was rumpled and damp, as were the grease-spattered T-shirt and jeans. His jaw was dark with shadow, his eyes weary and restless. He was a man in search of something, she realized with a heavy heart.

The breeze blew with little effect in the heat, other than to prickle the skin of her arms and neck. Brenna felt restless, too, hungry for something she couldn't name.

"We've had a lot of extra work at Avery's," Luke said at last. "Denny's staying late."

"Avery wouldn't attract the extra customers if you weren't there," Brenna said. "Everybody always wanted you to do the body work on their cars."

Luke shrugged and looked down. His wrists rested on his knees, the glass of tea dripping water onto the steps below. "Are you happy, Brenna?" he asked without looking at her. She felt her heart clench.

"I . . . suppose so." *When you're with me I'm happy.* She could have told him that, but she'd sworn not to burden him with that. She would let him go when she had to, and she would find the strength not to ask him to stay.

"You love your café, right?"

He raised his eyes to hers then, and she wanted to reach out and touch him when she saw the question there. Dear Lord, she thought. He needs my help somehow. She wanted to take away his misery, but she wasn't sure she could bridge the gap between them.

"Yes," she said. "I love the café, I love early morning here in this house and evening when the stars come out. I . . . love most things about my life." And she loved Luke.

"And the children," he prompted. "You love working with the children."

She nodded and Luke sighed, frowning as he stared across the field at the heat lightning. Brenna could feel lightning of a different sort, some raw emotion unleashed in Luke, and she sat tensely, waiting.

"Avery's a nice guy," he began. Then his breath stopped somewhere in his chest and the words died. "It's drudgery," he said at last, painfully. "I thought I could go back to working on cars full-time, but I hate it. It was always more of a hobby with me, and I guess I should have left it at that."

Brenna could feel a hard knot building in her stomach, fueling a spiraling fear. "What would you do?" she said in a low, hoarse voice, not daring to look at him.

"I'm going to talk to Jeff about working full-time with the kids at the center." There was a grim determination to his voice, as though he knew what her reaction would be.

Brenna's eyes flew to his face, but he was still staring out over the field. "The kids! Luke, whatever gave you an idea like that?"

"Is it so crazy?" His voice was ironic, and his gaze was lacerating. "Don't I like children, Brenna? Or am I so irresponsible that I don't belong with them?"

"It's nothing like that," she said hesitantly, wondering if in her heart it was. "It's just that . . . they try the patience sometimes, Luke. They won't ever do all the things a normal child does, and it can be heartbreaking to watch them try." Hesitantly, she added, "Clinton puts it more cruelly. He says they have no potential."

"I'm not Burgess, Brenna."

It was true. He and Clinton were as different as night and day, and yet . . . "Are you sure this isn't some kind of . . . penance, some duty you feel you have to perform?"

"And who would I be doing penance for, Brenna? You?" His voice was gravelly, his blue eyes relentless as they probed hers in the growing shadows.

"No," she said hoarsely. "We've both done our penance for what happened between us. This penance is for you. For not letting yourself have the things that might make you happy." She could feel herself trembling when she finished. It was so hard to say the things that were between them.

"What *would* make me happy, Brenna?" he asked softly, and still his eyes held her captive. "You?"

"I don't know," she whispered. "I truly don't know, Luke. But your life is full of all the times you went away. Don't hurt those kids, Luke. Don't let them learn to love you and then go away. They form attachments, and they... feel pain when someone leaves them." She was talking about herself as much as the children.

"Don't you think I feel pain, too?" he demanded, his voice scraping in his throat. "Don't you think that leaving has always hurt me, too? I'm not superhuman, Brenna. That's why I'm trying so hard to find what I need. The work and the..." But he didn't finish and say what it was he was looking so hard to find. Brenna felt that hard knot of fear rising to her throat. *Do you need me, Luke? Will you ever need me?*

She wanted to hold him and to kiss him and to make him take her upstairs to the bedroom, but she had no right to do any of those things with him, not when he was so obviously in this emotional pain.

He looked away from her then and pressed the glass against his forehead, letting drops of the condensed water run down his cheek and jaw. His eyes were closed, his jaw set in a grim line. "This isn't a whim, Brenna," he said. "I've worked toward something like this for a long time. I set up the support program in Iowa to help families on the race circuit."

"You can't fix people the way you fix cars," she said softly.

"Dammit, Brenna! You're not listening!" The glass landed on the grass below with a thud and strong fingers grasped her upper arms and turned her to face him. Her breath left her when she saw the look on his face, as though the heat lightning in the sky had somehow suffused his soul. "I went to college for this! I studied psychology and sociology and I worked my tail off. I got a teaching certificate because one time in high school you told me I'd make a good teacher. And I do, Brenna. I do! I'm good at it and I love it and I didn't spend that money you gave me on education so I could rebuild cars at Avery's garage!"

Her mouth opened, but no sound came out.

He was silent a long moment before his grip on her relaxed. "That was a hell of a way to say thanks for what you did, wasn't it?" he said grimly. Still his eyes sought hers, overwhelming her as though she were drowning in ocean depths. "Thank you, Brenna," he whispered.

"It was your money," she managed to say. "You gave me the house."

But he shook his head. "It was something you didn't have to do and it was nice," he said, not letting her belittle her gesture.

Somehow his hands on her arms had begun a caress, and the blue gaze holding hers gentled. "Come here," he murmured, pulling her against him until her head rested on his shoulder. "Just relax and try to pretend we can get along for more than five minutes at a time." She knew he was teasing her, and it made her smile.

"Brenna?" he asked softly after a bit.

"Hmm?"

"What we used to have between us, it's not all gone. It's different now, but it's there."

She didn't answer, content to take this moment when it was offered and find peace in his arms. Yes, there was something between them still. She didn't know how tenuous it was or how enduring, but she was willing to fight for it.

Sunday morning they left the sunshine behind in Illinois and drove to Iowa where dark clouds huddled together over the cornfields. Luke drove his car with Brenna in the front and Julie and a nervous Denny in the back. Denny had pleaded with Luke that morning to somehow get him out of this date, but Luke was adamant that it was time Denny stopped feeling sorry for himself and went out with a member of the opposite sex.

"She's about as opposite as you can get," Denny agreed miserably. "She wears more earrings than Avery." Julie, who had each ear pierced in three places, did, indeed, wear more earrings than Avery, who had only one ear pierced in two places. Brenna decided that pierced ears had somehow become a barometer of masculinity and femininity, but she wasn't sure how many equaled what. It was a complicated world when a woman worried she might appear too manly if she wore only two earrings. Brenna finally gave up worrying and wore her own set of pearl studs.

Denny had a bad habit of falling asleep when he was nervous, so he was snoring before they were halfway to Iowa. "Don't mind him," Luke assured Julie. "If he didn't like you he'd get car sick instead of falling asleep."

Julie seemed to take that piece of information in stride, and Brenna kept up a running patter of small talk the rest of the trip.

Without looking Luke reached behind his seat to poke Denny awake as the car turned into the track entrance. "Fine date you are," Luke chastised him, and Denny groaned and rubbed his head.

The corrugated metal fence around the track was painted with ads for motor oil, tires, spark plugs and other odds and ends Brenna didn't recognize. It had been ten years since she'd been to a track, and she felt Luke glancing at her as he paid their admission and parked the car.

"You want to go see the drivers?" Luke asked casually. Brenna nodded. She had come this far; she might as well get both feet wet. It was almost ten years since she'd been at a track, and she felt the familiar clenching in her chest as they approached the garage area where drivers and their crews milled about the cars, wielding wrenches and pliers and testing cables.

"Luke McShane, is that you?" a tall, thin man with graying hair asked in wonder as he straightened from the hood of a car.

Luke smiled and stuck out his hand. "How you doing, Bob?"

"Great! Just great! Hell, it's good to see you, Luke. You sort of dropped out of sight after you hit the wall. You racing today?"

Luke shook his head. "Just part of the audience today, Bob." He put one large hand on the back of Denny's neck and drew him forward. "You remember Denny Hammond, don't you? This is his sister Brenna and a friend, Julie."

Bob nodded and scrutinized Denny. "You were building a car for someone, weren't you?"

Denny shuffled his feet and cleared his throat. "Fact was, it didn't work out so well. I'm working in a little body shop in Illinois now."

"Hey, Bob!" a short man with a wrench in each hand called. "C'mere and take a look at this crankcase!"

"Yeah, yeah," Bob said, waving a hand over his shoulder. "Be right there." He pumped Luke's hand again. "You get back out here now, boy. A West Central Region champ don't just quit."

Brenna's smile stiffened and she avoided looking at Luke as they walked towards the stands. No, a champ didn't quit. Luke McShane wasn't a quitter. The words echoed in her head, words she'd heard over and over when they were first married. She was so proud of him when he brought that trophy home. But that trophy wasn't the final goal of his racing; it was only a spur that drove him on. The prize money was over ten thousand dollars that year, a slight profit when his expenses were figured. If it weren't for her café and his job at Avery's, they wouldn't have made it. Those were lean years, but Luke McShane was a champ. And every time the phone rang at night, Brenna wondered if someone was telling her that the champ had crashed into a wall. In the end it was one of the things she couldn't live with.

Yet Brenna felt something else here at the track. Listening to the people sitting around them in the stands, smelling the fresh dirt of the track and the oil that seemed to hang in the air, seeing the cars for the first race lining up, she felt a stirring, a fraction of the excitement Luke must have felt each time he climbed behind the wheel. She turned her head to glance at him and met serious blue eyes studying her as though something puzzled Luke. "Is it all right?" he asked quietly. "Us being here at the track—Can you handle it?"

She nodded. "It doesn't seem so scary now," she admitted. "I don't know why, but I never could stand to come here."

His large hand slipped over hers and squeezed, and he gave her a barely perceptible smile. "I missed you all those times I was racing," he admitted. "I'd look up in the stands and wish you were there."

She didn't have an answer to that. She looked back into time with the perspective of ten years and wondered at how lonely they had both been and how powerless to help each other. She felt anew the pain of not being there when he had crashed into the wall.

He was restless. She could feel it in him, and she knew he was trying to come to terms with something. He left them for a while, and Brenna kept scanning the track until she caught sight of him standing alone beside the fence, his fingers curled around the wire, his forehead leaning against it. Somebody must have recognized him because in a few minutes a small group of men had joined him, and Brenna could see Luke pull himself together and force a relaxed smile to his face.

When he returned, she stole surreptitious glances at him, wondering if he was all right but afraid to ask. He took her hand and they both held on as though to a lifeline. She told herself that she was here for him now, that the past was behind them. After a bit, she felt the tension ebb from him.

Later on, Brenna listened to Luke and Denny earnestly explaining the races to Julie, and she couldn't help smiling. Their voices were so much like her father when he was enthusing over his car. "This is the Bomber class," Luke was saying. "I got started driving in these races. The cars are basically right off the street, but you can't make more than about a hundred dollars for a night's racing."

"So you got a—what do you call it?—a souped up car?" Julie asked.

"Aw, hell, you shoulda seen it," Denny piped up. "Luke had this really hot number he helped build for the Late Model class. You gotta buy the chassis from a special company, and the whole car ends up running about twenty or thirty thousand dollars. But, man, could he compete in that thing."

Luke smiled to himself. One way to bring Denny out of his shell was to get him talking about cars, Luke thought with satisfaction as Julie asked more questions and Denny readily supplied the answers. Luke glanced at Brenna again, and when he saw that she was watching the race he took the opportunity to study her. She was so beautiful. He probably would have given up racing for her ten years ago if she'd asked. But she hadn't asked. Maybe if he hadn't gone back to racing after Dory died, or if Brenna had come with him on race nights... No, there was no point in reliving that. He'd given her grief enough. What had happened was over and they couldn't recapture the past. Or so he'd told himself a hundred times since he'd set eyes on her again. He couldn't stop thinking of making love to her, of how she'd felt so soft and warm and willing as they'd brought each other's bodies to that sweet mating. He felt things with

Brenna that he'd never felt with another woman, and he drew strength from her and peace.

When a woman behind him gave a loud shout of encouragement to one of the drivers, Luke came out of his trance and saw that Brenna was meeting his gaze head on, studying him as thoughtfully as he'd been studying her. They sat looking at each other a moment longer, then their fingers twined together and it was as though something unspoken had passed between them.

Denny and Julie hadn't stopped talking all during the races. When the last one was over and they were walking back to the car, Luke poked Brenna with his elbow and nodded toward them. Brenna smiled and shook her head in wonder.

Word had passed among the drivers that Luke McShane was on the grounds and a troupe of them caught up to him in the parking lot. Brenna stood off to the side, marveling at the respect they showed him, whether they were asking him a question about a car or filling him in on their families. Luke knew them all and all their children, and he asked about each and every one. This was the Luke that Brenna remembered from the better times, a man who tried to fix everything and everybody he touched.

Luke looked around for her, took her hand and pulled her into the circle with him, looping his arm over her shoulders, earning her the admiring glances of the men in their racing suits and grease-stained coveralls.

It was forty-five minutes before they could get away. They found Denny and Julie earnestly engaged in conversation as they leaned on the car. "Can't say as I remember a time when Denny Hammond wasn't interested in talking racing with a bunch of drivers," Luke observed just loudly enough as they drew close.

Denny straightened quickly and shuffled his feet in agitation. "Well, I didn't see any sense in wasting time," he said crisply. Luke grinned.

"Want to drive the car?" Luke asked Brenna lazily as he opened the passenger door.

She turned to face him with a frown. "And why would you ask something like that?"

"You sound suspicious, honey," he said, looking like he was trying hard not to grin at her.

"I am. You always had ulterior motives when you offered to let me drive your car."

"Me?" he said with an innocent raise of his eyebrows. "Name one time."

"Well, there was the time you couldn't drive because you'd pulled your shoulder pretty bad in an accident and you didn't want me to know about it. And then one time you'd been messing around with your car and you'd popped the passenger door and you had to hold it on with your arm outside the window and you wanted me to drive. And then—"

"Okay, okay!" Luke said, laughing. "I give up." He trotted around to the driver's side, shaking his head. Brenna eyed him suspiciously when he got in.

"So what are you up to now?" she demanded.

"Me, up to something?" he said, giving her a not-too-convincing performance of innocence. "Not me."

But he was, she was sure of it. And she discovered just what it was when he maneuvered the car through a maze of unfamiliar streets, assuring her all the while that this was a shortcut home and then stopped the car at a curb in front of an enormous hotel.

"This," he announced grandly to the passengers in the back seat, "is where Brenna and I spent our honeymoon."

"Luke!" Brenna cried in aggravation. "This isn't it!"

"Of course it is, honey," he said in a grievous tone. "Don't you remember?"

Julie leaned forward to get a better look. "Wow. Pretty nice place."

"This wasn't it," Brenna insisted. "We stayed in a tiny little motel with all of fifteen rooms and they were so small that we couldn't get into the bathroom at the same time."

"Unless we both got in the tub together, which we did," Luke added helpfully.

"And the walls were paper thin," Brenna went on, trying to ignore his smile. "Heavens, you could hear the couple next door when—" She broke off quickly, remembering just how much you could hear through those walls and how she and Luke had been on the receiving end of knowing looks when they went to breakfast the next morning. She frowned at the hotel again. "And, besides, Luke said the owners were retiring. Oh..." It struck her that this was, indeed, the right place, but the little motel just wasn't there anymore. "I forgot," she said. "You gave me the headboard because they were tearing the place down."

She felt a stab of sadness that their little motel was gone, and she was suddenly glad Luke had saved a piece of it for her. "All that's left is the headboard from our bed," she said with a catch in her voice.

"And our memories," he said gently. They were silent a moment, looking out at the nicely paved parking lot, and Brenna remembered the gravel lot in front of their motel. Then Luke started the car. "Well, we started our marriage right anyway," he said.

And we ended it in bitterness and misery, Brenna thought. Such a fine start to a marriage in that little hotel, and then such loneliness. She looked out the window, watching the sky darken as an afternoon shower built on the horizon.

"Hey!" Denny prompted from the back seat. "Take the old Kiefer Road home."

"It's dirt and gravel," Luke said.

"Yeah, but it hasn't rained, so it won't be soft. And it cuts thirty miles off the trip."

Luke shrugged, and Denny and Julie resumed their conversation in the back. Brenna stared out the window again, but she could feel Luke glancing at her often. Finally she turned her head and met his somber gaze.

"Why did I have to come back?" he said quietly, repeating her words from that other day when he'd given her the headboard. His eyes went back to the road before they skimmed her face again.

"Luke," Brenna said softly. "I didn't really mean it when I said that. It was just that...I didn't want to hurt anymore."

"I know," he said, and she knew he was weary with hurting, too. "I thought about that a lot since then. And I still don't have all the answers, Brenna. But I know I *did* have to come back, and it had to do with us, with what's still between us."

She had wanted his return to be because of her, and his answer gave her a measure of peace. Had they ever really been apart? she thought as she studied his strong profile. No, she had carried Luke McShane's memory in her heart all these years, had carried it fiercely and lovingly. But she wanted more than just memories for the next ten years. One broken heart was enough for a lifetime.

Nine

The drought had broken. Thunderstorms rolled over the fields every other day and the corn and soybeans surged toward the sky.

"A genuine, worm-burning, ball of fire homer!" Luke shouted as Eddie Haywood swung the bat with a grunt and sent the ball skittering through the infield of the empty lot behind the community center. Luke grinned as he waved Eddie around the bases, the boy's stout legs pumping vigorously. Eddie's mother, Charly, had just arrived in the van to take all the kids home and she stood on the sidelines, cheering her son and giving him a big hug when he crossed home plate.

Luke gathered the bats and gloves and herded the boys off the field. The wind was picking up and gray clouds blotted out the sun, the beginning of another afternoon storm.

It was a week since the races in Iowa, and, looking at Luke's easy grin, Brenna had to remind herself that Luke was still fighting his demons. Often she awoke in the night to the quiet click of the back door closing. And when she looked out her window into the dark, she saw him walking in the moonlight, pacing out his troubles in the wet grass.

"Brenna?" It was Jeff Markert, out of breath from trotting in from the outfield. He was frowning.

"What's wrong, Jeff?"

"Have you seen Mary?"

Brenna looked around, frowning. "She was standing by that tree over there." At five, Mary was the youngest in the program and the newest member. She was still painfully shy and preferred watching the boisterous baseball games from the sidelines.

"We're going to have to find her fast," Jeff said. "That storm's going to be here in half an hour. You help Charly get the kids in the van, and I'll get Luke. Tell Charly I'll drive Mary home myself."

Charly didn't want to take off with the kids until Mary was found, but Brenna convinced her that it would be best to get them home before the storm hit. Brenna grabbed her sweater and Luke's sweatshirt from her car, and then caught up with Luke and Jeff behind the building.

"Brenna and I will follow the creek," Luke said, taking the sweatshirt from Brenna.

"I'm going to call Mary's mother," Jeff said. "Then I'll head straight out across the field. Take shelter if you can't get back here when the storm hits."

Luke nodded and set off, Brenna tugging on her sweater in his wake. The wind was whipping her hair around her face, the temperature was dropping rapidly. They walked quickly and silently, scanning the edges of the small stream and stopping to call Mary's name in the face of the rising wind.

The thought that something might have happened to Mary gave Brenna chills, and she could see the same worried fear shadowing Luke's face. Grimly, she walked faster to keep up with Luke.

She was so intent on the search that she didn't realize where they were until they pushed through some cedar trees and wild roses by the stream to clamber down the bank. Brenna saw that they were at a bend in the stream where the water was so shallow that it was barely a trickle over a bed of pebbles and small stones. One side of the bank was dirt and rock, the other a steep limestone cut, riddled with openings almost covered in ferns. Oak and elm trees, their roots protruding from the bank like dried rope, formed a canopy of leaves over the stream. It was a place where Brenna and Luke used to come to talk quietly together after school. It was their own private place, a place she hadn't seen for years. She glanced quickly at Luke, but he was absorbed in looking at the soft mud of the bank.

"Here are some footprints!" he said. "Come on!"

He ran fleetly over the stones, with Brenna trying to keep up with him and not fall. She rounded the corner just behind him, stopping short when he called Mary's name.

Brenna saw the little girl sitting cross-legged under a huge elm tree on the bank, leaning over and carefully plucking wild violets. She looked up, startled, when she heard her name, and then her lower lip began to quiver and the tears flowed down her face. "Mo-o-o-o-m," she whimpered, rocking back and forth.

Brenna reached the girl just behind Luke, and both knelt in front of her. "It's all right, honey," Brenna murmured over and over, stroking the girl's brown hair. "Don't cry."

Luke gently turned Mary's chin up and smiled. "See, Mary. It's just Brenna and Luke. You remember us from the Center, don't you?"

Mary shook her head, but Luke assured her that she'd remember them if she tried, and Mary looked from one to the other. "Okay," she said at last, and Brenna smiled.

It was beginning to rain, hard drops that always preceded a real squall. Brenna looked around, seeking some kind of shelter. They'd never get back to the Center before the storm hit in full force.

She looked at the elm tree again, and memory hit her like a blow. This was the elm where she and Luke came one night after the movies. This was where they lay in the grass in each other's arms. This was where they conceived Dory.

She looked at Luke over Mary's head and his eyes met hers. Such soulful, aching blue eyes. And in those eyes she saw that he remembered, too. His gaze held hers a second longer, and then he turned his attention back to Mary.

"Come on, honey," he said. "Let's find someplace to stay dry until the storm's over." He stood with Mary in his arms and picked his way down the bank to the stream, Brenna following. It was raining harder now, and all around them the wind danced in a frenzy, whipping the tree branches into a froth of twisting leaves.

Luke found an opening in the limestone bluff that was large enough for the three of them. He went into the cave first, hunkering down with Mary against his chest, holding out his hand to help Brenna.

She crawled in beside him and sat down in the remaining tiny space, her knees drawn up to keep her legs from getting wet as the rain lashed the rock around the opening. Her hip was pressed against Luke's thigh, and she could hear his harsh breathing in the confines of the cave.

Mary, wearing only a thin T-shirt and shorts, began shivering. Luke struggled to pull off his sweatshirt in the limited space, then pulled it over Mary's head. "Put your head back, honey, and go to sleep," Luke told her softly when she yawned.

She did as he said, but her eyes forced themselves open just as she seemed on the verge of sleep. She looked up into Luke's face, scrutinizing him worriedly. "No leave me?" she asked.

Luke shook his head. "No leave you," he agreed. Apparently satisfied, the little girl settled back again and was soon fast asleep.

Brenna's gaze drifted to Luke's, and she couldn't keep the same question from her own face. She ached with the need she felt for him, an ache made more wrenching by her conviction that it was only a matter of time before he would be gone from her life.

Luke glanced down at the sleeping Mary, then murmured softly, "It hasn't been easy, has it, Brenna?" She shook her head wearily, and he said, "We fight and we make love and we work to understand each other. We always have, I think." He had turned his eyes to the rain outside the cave, but now he looked at her. "I'm not going to make any promises I can't keep, Brenna. Sometimes I get an urge to feel the road under me and hear the engine whine while I see how fast I can push it. But it's not as strong as it used to be. I want you to know I'm trying. I know how much you hate the racing and . . . and I want you to be happy."

Her throat was constricted and her voice sounded hoarse. "Isn't it silly?" she whispered, trying to smile. "We want to make each other happy, and we end up being lonely instead."

His fingers reached out and touched her cheek, and in the damp coolness of the cave they were warm and comforting. "I want you to do something for me," he said gently.

"What?" Her eyes searched his face.

"I want you to stop worrying."

"Why don't you just ask me to fly?" she said wryly.

He smiled at that, though his eyes were still solemn. His fingers stroked her cheek. "We've had enough unhappiness, you and I. Let's not let any more bitterness for what might have been come between us. I want to know you don't hate me."

"My God, no, Luke! I could never hate you."

"What then?"

She looked into his eyes again and felt that familiar ache. She wanted to tell him she loved him. It was something that cried to be said. But she couldn't. The words would be like a chain on Luke, asking him stay whether he wanted to or not. She wouldn't hold him like that.

"I don't want you to be unhappy," she said simply, deliberately not telling him what he wanted to know.

Luke let his fingers linger on her face as he studied her, then he abruptly dropped his hand and looked out at the sky. "The rain's let up," he said. "Let's get Mary back before everyone's frantic."

Luke had been pensive for the two days since they'd found Mary. Brenna had often glanced out a window of the house in the evening to see him bending over the hood of either his car or hers. But usually he wasn't working, just leaning there lost in thought. He spent more time at the hospital with his father now, and he was tired and dejected when he got home.

Now as she drove back to Waldo from Cedar Crest, the nearest town some twenty miles away, she was lost in thoughts of her own. Today would have been Dory's tenth birthday.

Brenna turned into the gravel road to the cemetery, slowing her car. The day was hot, the air so still that everything seemed to move in slow motion. She crested the hill that overlooked Dory's grave and saw Luke's car parked under the shade of a large oak tree.

He hadn't heard her car yet. He was standing at Dory's grave, his back to the road, his arms folded over his chest. Brenna felt hot tears prick her eyes, and she took her time parking her car behind his. She wanted to be sure she could talk to him without crying. She carefully slid the package from the Cedar Crest pharmacy under the seat, then picked up the bouquet of daisies she'd brought and started toward the grave.

He turned his head and watched her walk slowly and carefully to his side. She's so pretty, he thought. She should never have had to lose her baby. Our baby. She looked so delicate in that soft pink blouse and matching skirt, and her hair tumbled down in abandon. She looked the same as she did ten years before, except for that sadness in her eyes. God, he'd do anything to erase that sadness! He'd done the best he could before, leaving her ten years ago when she seemed to grow more unhappy each time she looked at him. And yet, that seemed to have done nothing to ease her pain. He didn't know what he should have done. He didn't know what he should do now, either. He would cause her pain if he left and pain if he stayed.

She stopped beside him, her eyes never leaving his face, and slid her hand into his when he held it out to her.

"I didn't expect you...to remember," she said questioningly.

"She was my daughter, my only child," he said, the slightest tremble in his voice. "I couldn't ever forget her birthday."

They stood there silently a long while, and finally Brenna bent to arrange the daisies in the marble container in front of the tombstone. "The whole time I was pregnant I used to think about how wonderful my baby's life was going to be," she said, standing up. "And I would picture this beautiful child picking daisies in the summer, and I'd arrange them in a pitcher and put them in my child's bedroom." Her voice cracked then, despite her resolve not to lose control. "I never thought I'd be bringing daisies to her grave."

Luke's hand clasped hers, and the next instant she flung herself into his arms. They held on to each other desperately, clinging together to weather the grief. When Brenna finally dared to look up at him, she saw the tears on his face. He took a deep breath and wiped at them with the back of his other hand, and she saw what he was holding—a teddy bear.

Luke met her eyes and this time made no attempt to shield his hurt and loneliness from her. "I didn't have any idea what ten-year-old girls like," he said, almost apologetically, and Brenna loved him more than ever in that moment. "I never got to know her. I never even got to tell her how much I already loved her."

"I'm sure she knew," Brenna assured him gently. "You used to sing to her when you came to bed at night. You'd put your head down beside my stomach and sing the most beautiful lullabies to her." Her voice broke again, and Luke gathered her tightly against him.

Brenna's body shook with the force of her sobs, and when she reached up to Luke, she felt the tears on his face again. When she could manage her voice, she whispered, "Let's go home."

He pulled away from her gently and then knelt beside the grave, propping the teddy bear against the tombstone.

"It won't last, Luke," she said, feeling a rising tide of helplessness. "The rain will ruin it."

"It'll ruin the daisies, too," he said, standing up. "But we have to give her something. It's her birthday."

He put his arm around Brenna and they stood looking down at the grave before they silently walked back to their cars.

Luke was waiting for Brenna when she closed up the Chestnut Tree Café the next night. "Hi," he said softly as he pushed himself away from where he'd been leaning against his car. "I thought maybe you'd go see a movie with me." He hesitated a moment, his face betraying that he was unsure of himself, and he added, "If you want to."

Brenna smiled. "I want to. Thanks."

Loraine came around the building from locking the back door, and stopped when she saw Luke. "You two young folks have plans for tonight?" she asked briskly, then shook her head without waiting for an answer. "It's none of my business, but you two need to get out more. You both work too hard. You know what they say. All work and no play is a sailor's delight."

Brenna saw Luke look quickly at the ground to hide his smile. "Thank you for that bit of wisdom, Loraine."

"Well, you're welcome," Loraine said. "I'll stop by your house on the way home if you want, Brenna, and tell Denny your car is here."

"Okay. Thanks."

"Here's the plan," Luke said as he helped her into his car. "Two Elvis Burgers followed by the silliest movie we can find anywhere around."

"A good plan," Brenna concurred. "In fact, a great plan, especially if you throw in a couple of hot-fudge sundaes at the end."

"You got it," Luke said, and he gave her a smile as he pulled the car onto the highway.

Luke delivered on his plan. The Elvis Burgers were followed by a drive to Cedar Crest, where they watched a detective movie spoof. They were both still laughing when they came outside, and Luke put his arm around her shoulder. "Ready for that hot-fudge sundae?" Luke asked, smiling down at her.

"Hmm-hmm," she said.

"Anything the lady wants," he said. "Tonight is your night."

"My, but aren't we accommodating?" she teased him, and he rewarded her with another smile. "You aren't going to go and give me a string of presents and end up with something like my headboard tonight, are you?"

Luke shook his head. "Not those kind of presents anyway. I thought it might make you happy to have a night out just for you and me."

"It does," she told him. "I'm having a wonderful time." She smiled at him across the dark car, and he reached out and took her hand, enveloping it in his larger one.

He was such a handsome man, she thought as a street-lamp washed pale light across his face as they passed it. So strong and yet gentle. She would never forget the tender way he'd laid the teddy bear at Dory's grave. And now he was doing this for her, giving her a night when she could put aside her sadness.

Brenna had felt a measure of peace since they faced their grief together yesterday at the cemetery and gave each other the comfort they'd failed to give ten years ago.

Forty-five minutes later they pulled into the driveway, contented with each other and replete with hot-fudge sundaes. The moon was full as Luke parked the car, and the night was still except for the hum of crickets and the buzzing of insects against the front porch screen where the porch light burned.

"Denny must be out," Brenna said lazily, nodding toward the porch light.

"You want to stay out here awhile?" Luke asked. She nodded.

He turned on the radio and found a station playing oldies. They sat there in silence listening to the music until a slow tune came on. Without speaking, Luke turned and held out his hands to her. She took them and he drew her across the seat and outside into the night.

The grass was wet with dew, and Brenna slid out of her sandals. She stood in the moonlight before him, barefoot and in a white dress, her hair loose and moving slightly in the breeze.

Luke had dressed up for her tonight in white cotton pants and a black, short-sleeved shirt. He looked devastating in the moonlight with his black hair and devilish blue eyes. Brenna looked up at him and let her eyes languidly drift half closed.

Luke drew her into his arms so slowly and tenderly that Brenna felt her heart begin to throb in yearning. She wanted him so. And now, with the soft music from the radio, the magic of a summer night, and Luke McShane holding her like this, Brenna felt as though she really might have him, as though the world was starting anew for them.

"Luke," she said softly when the song ended and they continued dancing slowly in the wet grass to the next one. "You never married and you never had children."

"No."

"I always pictured you with children of your own. You would have been so good with them."

Luke was silent for so long that Brenna thought he wasn't going to answer. But then he said, "I often thought about children, but...there wasn't anybody I wanted to have them with."

Tell him, her heart urged. It's the right time.

The song was over and their dance came to a stop with both of them just holding each other, their eyes meeting and catching. Luke whispered her name, and his head bent down as he pressed his forehead to hers before his mouth found hers. His hands moved restlessly over her back, and Brenna leaned into him, loving the hard feel of his body and his male smell.

They pulled apart slowly and reluctantly when a car pulled into the drive, its lights sweeping over them. "Denny," Brenna said with a sigh when she recognized the car.

They stood together, watching as the car kicked up gravel in its haste, and Brenna briefly wondered what was chasing Denny now. When it slid to a stop, both doors flew open simultaneously, and Denny and Julie jumped out. "Luke!" Julie called, and Brenna knew from her voice that something was wrong. "We've been looking for you! Get to the hospital. Your dad...it's not good."

Brenna hurried to the other side of Luke's car as he jumped in and started the engine. As he maneuvered around Denny's car and then sped down the drive, Brenna knew she couldn't tell him now what she'd been about to in the moonlight—the pregnancy-test kit she'd bought at the Cedar Crest pharmacy showed positive. They were going to have another baby.

Ten

It always seemed that the sky was gray and overcast for a funeral, Brenna thought sadly. It had been like this when they buried Dory. She glanced at Luke. He was sitting next to her, but he hadn't looked at her either during the church service or now, during the interment. The canopy covering the grave and the mourners cast even deeper shadows on his face.

It was three days since Luke had been summoned to the hospital. He and Brenna had kept vigil at James's bedside until he had died toward morning, his hand holding his son's.

James's brother, John, came from Minnesota immediately, and now as the service concluded, Luke stood and said a few words to his uncle. Brenna waited while Luke moved among the mourners, inviting them to the funeral luncheon Loraine had prepared back at Brenna's house. After he'd said a word or two to each person, he came back to Brenna and still without meeting her eyes, took her hand and walked slowly toward the car.

James McShane was well liked by everyone in Waldo, and a crowd was already gathering when Luke, John and Brenna reached the house. Luke guided his car past those already in the drive and parked by the garage. Brenna hadn't had any time alone with Luke since the night James died, and now she could feel grief separating them again. Luke turned to look at her, and she saw some fleeting desperation in his eyes, something she'd seen when Dory died.

The mood inside the house wasn't as somber as at the funeral service. Small groups of people gathered with their plates of food and remembered the good times they'd had with James. Brenna left Luke and John with the Conley brothers—accompanied by their wives this time—and headed for the kitchen to help Loraine.

Brenna had gotten up early that morning to bake rolls and several cherry pies, while nibbling crackers to hold her morning sickness at bay. As she was leaving for the funeral home, Loraine had arrived with potato salad and macaroni-and-cheese and had taken charge of the two hams to be baked.

Brenna picked up a bowl of potato chips that was nearly empty and carried it into the kitchen.

Loraine looked up and frowned. "You look completely tuckered out. Why don't you go lie down?"

Brenna shook her head. She felt as exhausted as she looked, but she needed to keep busy to take her mind off James's death and the haunted look she'd seen on Luke's face. So she didn't let herself take any time to think, just carried dishes of food back and forth from the kitchen, stopping to say a word here and there and trying not to look for Luke.

Denny and Julie were in a corner talking to the Hennesys, and Brenna lingered a moment to watch Denny. She marveled at the changes in him since Luke had taken it upon himself to thrust him together with Julie. Denny had a settled air about him, a quiet assurance. Unconsciously, Brenna's gaze strayed to the other side of the room and collided with Luke's. They looked at each other over the heads of the crowd, and then somebody said something to Luke and caught his attention. Restless, Brenna went back to the kitchen.

It was late afternoon and the people were trickling away when someone tapped hesitantly on the back door. Brenna answered it. Clinton stood there, looking sad and uncomfortable.

"Brenna," he said, and then he cleared his throat. "I just came to tell you how sorry I am. About everything. Luke's dad and . . . and the things I said to you before."

"It's all right, Clinton. Come on in."

He stood just inside the kitchen door, his hands firmly anchored in his pockets, obviously unsure of his reception and not quite able to look Brenna in the eye. He cleared his throat again. "I just want to wish you the best of luck, Brenna. I can't honestly say I'm happy over you and Luke getting back together, but I . . . well, I guess all these years I knew it was never really over between you two."

Loraine came to Brenna's rescue, turning up at her side and saying, "There's plenty of food in there, Clinton. Go help yourself."

He nodded, took one more look at Brenna, then said, "I'd like to offer my condolences to Luke." Brenna followed him to the kitchen doorway, watching as he crossed the room, pumping hands in his habitual fashion until he reached Luke. Brenna couldn't make out what Clinton said, but Luke nodded gravely and shook his hand. On the point of falling asleep from exhaustion, she turned back to Loraine and said, "I think I might go lie down awhile. Call me if you need help."

"That'll be the day when I can't manage to feed a few people," Loraine groused, looking down at the ham she was slicing, but Brenna caught the concern in her eyes.

Brenna woke up to a twilight gray that left her disoriented. She turned over on her side and saw that she was in her own bedroom, now shadowed with coming nightfall. She was wearing her short pink robe over her bra and panties, and she was lying on top of the bedspread. Somebody was moving quietly in front of her dresser, and she started to sit up in alarm until she recognized Luke's familiar form.

He turned and saw that she was awake. "I'm sorry," he murmured. "I didn't mean to wake you up."

Brenna saw that he was holding the white dress shirt he'd just removed. "What are you doing here?" she murmured sleepily, the question sounding vaguely familiar to her, an echo from another day.

Slowly he tossed the shirt onto the dresser and came to sit on the edge of the bed. "Everybody's gone home," he said. "Denny's gone somewhere with Julie, and Loraine said she'd come back tomorrow morning to clean up the dishes." A ghost of a smile shadowed his mouth. "I have orders not to let you anywhere near the dishes."

Brenna smiled. She couldn't keep her gaze from drifting up Luke's naked torso and surveying his handsome face. When she married him, he was her idea of the most gorgeous man in the world. Time hadn't altered that opinion. "You must be tired," she said, taking in the weary lines around his eyes.

He nodded. "I thought I'd lie down and rest for a while. I came in here because . . . I needed to be near you."

"Come on," she said in a husky voice, scooting over and patting the bed beside her. Luke kicked off his shoes and lay down, his arms laced under his head. Pensively, he stared up at the ceiling and they remained in silence as the dusky evening closed in around them, the cry of a mourning dove echoing in the stillness.

"When I was a kid," Luke said after a while, "Dad and I used to go to the races on a night like this. He knew some of the guys on the circuit, and he'd take me down to the drivers' area to meet them. When I started racing myself, he'd come every night he could, and he'd stand around by the cars and chew the fat with everyone. He never said he was proud, but I could see it in the way he'd watch every little detail before a race. And when I'd pull on my helmet, he'd come over and rap his knuckles on it. 'Such a hard head,' he'd say. And we'd both laugh. It was something he'd said as long as I can remember and I always looked forward to that moment when his eyes would twinkle and he'd say it." Luke took a hard, shaky breath and a mockingbird joined its song to the dove's in the tree outside. "He won't ever say that to me again, Brenna. I know it's a stupid thing to miss, but—"

His voice abruptly broke, and when she looked at him she saw the sheen of moisture in his eyes. She and Luke had gone through so much, she thought as she stretched out a hand and stroked his cheek in comfort. Triumphs and losses and joy and anguish, like all men and women. And somehow they were still struggling to hold on to each other no matter what the cost. There was something enduring between them, something worth fighting for.

He turned his head to the side to look at her, and she could see such yearning in his face that she cradled his head and leaned over to kiss him.

"Hold me," he whispered on a ragged plea. "Let me love you, Brenna. Put your arms around me and let me bury myself in you. You're so beautiful . . ."

The words died on his lips as his mouth took hers in a testament to his need. Brenna's arms tightened around him, bringing his hard male body up against her softer, yielding one. A hammering need pounded through her, as unrelenting and unstoppable as rising floodwaters. A groan escaped her as the force of it swept over her. They had always wanted each other like this, always physically, and now something deeper was calling to them both. Brenna could feel the alteration in the way Luke stroked her hair and slid the robe from her shoulders. This was what should have been between them ten years ago, this tender vulnerability that made them so much more than lovers. This was a true mating, a man and woman coming together to give everything of themselves in this one act.

Luke drew back long enough to look into Brenna's face, and she saw the reserve fall away from him, his feelings for her showing starkly and poignantly in those deep blue eyes.

They undressed each other and touched each other's bodies tenderly and hungrily and with infinite wonder. Brenna thought fleetingly that if she never had Luke McShane again in this lifetime she would remember this night forever for its mingling of sadness and—despite the mourning—beauty.

When he brought their bodies together at last and they strained to pleasure each other, Brenna felt that the stars whirled in their orbit and the moon rose over the house just for her and Luke. She cried out his name when the pleasure became more than she could bear, and he murmured love words to her again and again until the aloneness disappeared along with the pain and sadness. They lay holding each other afterward, damp with perspiration and spent, but each with a measure of peace.

Luke brushed his fingertips over Brenna's lips and kissed her shoulder before he slept. But Brenna lay awake, beset by old fears. She loved him so much. Grief might break her this time if he left. If he left... Their lovemaking tonight had been an affirmation. But what had they affirmed—a beginning or an end?

He was gone in the morning when she woke up. It might have all been a dream but for his white shirt still lying on her dresser. As soon as she put one foot on the floor, Brenna's stomach rolled with the first wave of nausea and she hurried to the bathroom to throw up. When the worst was over, she pulled on a robe and went downstairs to find some crackers to nibble.

She was sitting morosely at the kitchen table, staring at the stack of dirty bowls and pans in the sink, when the back door swung open and Loraine walked in, stopping short when she saw Brenna.

"What are you doing up already?" Loraine demanded.

"What do you mean, what am I doing up?" Brenna said. "I've got to get to the café as usual."

"Fergie and I can take care of the breakfast crowd. You need your rest." Loraine briskly set her purse on the counter and began running water in the sink.

"And why do I need to rest?" Brenna demanded peevishly.

Loraine turned around and faced her with a frown. "You've been through a lot with the funeral and all. And . . . you're pregnant, aren't you?"

Brenna stared, dumbfounded. "How did you know?"

"You're as like a daughter to me as any child I could have had," Loraine said stubbornly. "They say blood is thicker than soup, and I suppose that's so. It just seems to me you could have told me."

"I haven't even told Luke," Brenna said.

"What!"

Brenna shook her head. "He hasn't given me any guarantees that he's going to stay around this time, and I'm not going to hold him here by dangling a baby in front of him."

"He has a right to know," Loraine said, more kindly now. "After last time . . . he needs to be told."

"I know." Brenna took a deep breath and bit into another cracker. "Maybe I'll go by Avery's and tell him today."

It took her most of the morning to get her stomach settled enough to put on a pink cotton sundress and sandals. Loraine had gone to the café, assuring Brenna that everything was under control. Brenna drove to the local hardware store and under the tight-lipped scrutiny of Jason Conley, who said he was getting a new lunchpail, she bought a teddy bear.

She sat in her car a long time just looking at the teddy bear and trying to make herself go see Luke. She kept asking herself what he was thinking when he left her side this morning. When she finally pulled into the gravel drive leading to Avery's garage she was tense and edgy and she kept rehearsing lines in her head.

Avery came out of the garage wiping his hands on his coveralls, then smoothing down his full black beard. When he recognized Brenna he leaned in her car window and smiled broadly. "You finally gonna let me overhaul this junker?" he asked amiably.

"Not today," she told him, making an effort to smile back. "I was looking for Luke."

"Oh." Avery's face fell and he rubbed his hairy chin. "Didn't he tell you? He quit this morning." At Brenna's look, he shrugged. "Yeah. Told me he was sorry he couldn't give me any notice, but Denny would pick up the slack."

Brenna didn't remember what she said to Avery or how she made her exit, but she broke the speed limit all the way home. Her heart began thudding painfully when she saw Luke's car in the drive. All she could think of was Luke's sad eyes when he'd lain down with her last night. What hadn't he told her?

The house was silent and she could hear her painfully loud breathing in the empty kitchen. She heard a thump above and began climbing the stairs.

She stood silently in his open doorway, her heart constricting when she saw the open suitcase on the bed. Luke was folding shirts, and when he turned he saw her and stopped. The rest of the shirts dropped carelessly onto the bed and he took a step toward her, stopping when she stiffened.

"Brenna," he said, "listen to me—"

Her anger erupted then. "Listen to you?" she hissed. "Listen to you sweeten the goodbyes? Or were you planning to leave without saying anything?"

"It's not like that!" he said, his own anger rising to match hers. "I'm not leaving!"

Her eyes moved pointedly to the suitcase. "Then you're just changing bedrooms?" she said sarcastically.

"No! Listen!" He swore and moved to her swiftly, taking her shoulders despite her attempt to shrug away. "This is something I have to do, Brenna. I have to do one more race, just to prove to myself that I can after the accident. I'm going to Iowa for a couple of weeks. Denny and I are going to build race cars after we get some backing, and I'm going to drum up some sponsors. I'm going to race a week from Saturday. One race, Brenna, just one."

His fingers pressed into her shoulders, his voice pressed just as hard into her heart.

"How many times have you left this house for just one race?" she demanded bitterly. "And then it was one more after that and one more after that. There's no end to it, Luke."

"Dammit, Brenna! Aren't you listening? I'm coming back! I've talked to Jeff about my working full-time at the Center and it looks promising. But I've got to do this one last race."

"Then go do it," she said in a leaden voice. "Go do all the races you want, Luke. I won't stop you."

"Brenna," he whispered, trying to see into her face. "Don't let me go with this between us."

But she shook her head. "There's nothing between us now, Luke. Go on. Go." She pulled away from him and hurried down the hall, feeling stormy blue eyes following her. She didn't stop until she got to her car, and then she drove aimlessly, not even caring where she went. When she finally looked around to see where she was, she saw the cemetery coming up on her right. As though driven there by some demon, she pulled the car into the entrance and stopped. She took two deep, gulping breaths, and when she glanced at the car seat and saw the teddy bear she began to cry in great, wracking sobs.

"Drink this," Loraine ordered, thrusting a glass at Brenna.

"What is it?" Brenna muttered resignedly, taking the cold glass and sniffing the orangish liquid. "Smells good." It was five days since Luke had gone and Brenna's morning sickness inflicted even more misery on her.

"Of course it does. You think I'm fixing to poison you? It's apricot nectar. Best thing for morning sickness. Now sip it, then rest. Your daddy's downstairs and he wants to come up and see you."

"Daddy? Oh, heavens! He doesn't know I'm pregnant, does he? He probably wonders why I'm in bed and not at the café."

"Now calm down and sip," Loraine insisted sternly. "He don't know you're pregnant. I told him you were tired and your allergies was acting up. He just wants to talk to you about your cooking some fancy luncheon for Bishop Barbara."

"What's Daddy gone and done now?" Brenna asked. "This isn't some kind of engagement party, is it?"

"No, no, no. Your daddy's not about to marry the Bishop. This is just some to-do for her fancy friends and their bridge club. She wants it fast—two days from now on Saturday—and she's been buttering up your daddy to sweet talk you into doing it for her. Now, Fergie and I've got the menu all planned out, so you just say yes to your daddy and smile nice, hear?''

Brenna sighed and nodded, and Loraine studied her with a frown. ''Brenna, I know this isn't any of my business, but that's never stopped me before.''

Brenna could sense what was coming, and she stared down at the bedspread, plucking at it with her fingers.

''Honey, Luke's been gone off somewhere for five days now, and you've been drooping lower than my considerable bosom when I take off my bra. So I figure you two had some kind of spat. So I'll come right out and ask. Is it over the baby?''

Brenna shook her head. ''No, I didn't tell him.''

''Oh, laws,'' Loraine sniffed, shaking her head. ''Somebody ought to write an instruction book for young people. Just might do it myself. When you're young and foolish you value your pride over your happiness. You get old and a little smarter and you figure out pride can't keep you warm at night. Honey, you let Luke get away and you'd better buy yourself a heckuva big blanket. Now, finish that glass and I'll let your daddy come up.''

When Saturday morning rolled around, Brenna found herself facing the daunting task of helping Loraine and Fergie with their menu for Barbara's party. But she couldn't keep her mind on the job at hand, and twice Fergie found her daydreaming while his cream-puff shells nearly burned. Fergie was extremely sensitive about his cooking and he was so provoked that he shooed Brenna out to the counter to help Loraine fold napkins.

''Got the heave-ho, did you?'' Loraine asked knowingly. She watched Brenna absently fold a paper napkin with the design inside, and she put her hand over Brenna's, halting her. ''Why don't you go home, honey?''

Brenna shook her head. ''I'd rather keep busy.''

"If you keep on keeping busy like this, you're going to wreck the Bishop's party for sure. Everything went okay at the doctor's yesterday, didn't it?" she demanded worriedly.

Brenna nodded. "He said everything looks fine. And to stop worrying."

"Easy advice for a man," Loraine said dryly. "Now here—" she pushed a bowl of fresh vegetables across the counter to Brenna "—make those cute geese you do for parties."

Brenna went to work on the squash, carrots and radishes, using a paring knife and toothpicks to make animals. Her mind kept drifting, and she glanced at her watch. Luke would be racing today in Iowa. She couldn't shake the image of him looking into the stands of people, searching for a familiar face.

The bell over the door rang, and Cloris and Thaddeus Hennesy walked in, Cloris wiping her forehead with her arm. "I swear it's hot," she said. "Going to rain though."

"When we was in the UFO they put some kind of radio in Cloris's head and she always knows when it's going to rain," Thaddeus contributed knowingly.

"Too bad that there radio don't predict something useful, like when somebody's going to come to their senses," Loraine grumbled with a pointed look at Brenna.

Brenna barely heard her, her mind still at the race track. She was trying to remember why she had so stubbornly refused to go with Luke all those times in the past. What had she been so afraid of? *That he loved racing more than he loved her.* Racing, in Brenna's heart, was Luke's mistress, and pride kept Brenna from acknowledging it. She had feared that one day he wouldn't come back from the track, and so they had never reached out to each other, had never given totally, had never bridged the emotional chasm between them. But racing had always been second in Luke's heart to Brenna, and he'd told her as much if she'd only listened. She saw it now in the way he'd made love to her, the way he tried so hard to reach that hurt place inside her when he came back, the way he had gently awakened her to life again. And now he was alone at the track and she was here.

Brenna dropped the paring knife with a clatter and pushed aside the vegetables. She pulled off her apron and grabbed her purse.

"Lordy, what are you up to?" Loraine asked in astonishment.

"I'm going to Iowa," Brenna announced. She pushed open the door and called back over her shoulder, "If I take the Kiefer Road shortcut I can get there before Luke's race is over."

"Well, praise the Lord!" Loraine exulted behind her.

Cloris rushed to the door as Brenna was getting in the car. "You be careful on that Kiefer Road!" she called out. "Thaddeus and me, we've seen some strange things in the sky over that road and it weren't swamp gas!"

Suitably warned against aliens, Brenna picked up the teddy bear she'd left in the car and sat him down in the passenger seat. "You keep an eye out for UFOs," she advised him as she pulled onto the highway.

Her car was cursed. Brenna was sure of it. Here she was on Kiefer Road, somewhere between Waldo and the Iowa race track, in the middle of a raging downpour—Cloris's radio-receiving head was right after all—and her damn car had died.

Thunder had cracked and lightning had flashed for three hours now, the car had shown no signs of life and not a single car had passed. Apparently she was the only person in the entire county dim-witted enough to use this blasted road, she decided morosely. She checked her watch and cursed. Luke's race would be over by now, and no doubt he was on his way to another track. She'd never find him now.

She rummaged in the car until she found some nourishment in the glove compartment—a peanut-and-caramel candy bar. Old, stale nourishment at best. Then she fell into an exhausted sleep as the rain beat a tattoo on the car.

She woke up at dusk to a frantic tapping on her window. Brenna sat up straight, looked out the window and nearly passed out. It was still raining, her window was fogged and she could see some kind of creature resembling a hulking bear trying to peer in. Her first thought was that Cloris had warned her and would now have another story for that magazine—how a small-town café owner was kidnapped by Bigfoot.

She started to yell at the creature to frighten it away when she realized it was calling her name and it was most agitated.

"Who are you?" she demanded suspiciously, rolling down the window a crack.

"Brenna! It's me—Luke! Honey, I've been worried sick about you!"

"Luke?" she repeated dumbly, rubbing her eyes to clear them. It was indeed Luke, she saw when she rolled the window down. Luke dressed in a flapping black poncho and hood that accounted for the Bigfoot appearance.

"Lord, Brenna! Am I glad to see you! I got home and you weren't there, and I was scared to death you'd gone off and left like you did the other time. I went tearing up to your dad's place, but he hadn't seen you. Then I found Loraine and she said you were on your way to see me. I called the track, but no one had seen you. I've never been so scared in my life." He took a deep breath, his blue-eyed gaze searching her for injury. "Honey?" he said haltingly. "You think you could either open the door or roll down the window a tad more so I can get inside and talk to you. I'm half-drowned as it is."

"Yes! Luke, yes!" She was so addled she was doing both at the same time—rolling down the window and trying to unlock the door. Finally Luke was inside and she was scooting over to the passenger seat. She was sitting on the teddy bear, and she pulled it out from under her and held it. "Luke, this damn car is headed for the junk yard!" she swore. "It's stranded me for the last time!"

She was going on about the car and about Kiefer Road and about UFOs, but she saw that Luke was grinning at her. He'd thrown back his hood, and his handsome face and hair were wet with the rain. "What are you smiling about?" she demanded.

"You were coming to see me at the track," he said. "You've never done that, honey."

"If you're going to race, you're going to need a cheering section," she said with great dignity. "How did the race go?" She scanned his face anxiously. "Are you all right?"

"I'm fine, honey," he assured her. "I was pretty shaky when I got in the car, but...I thought about you and about coming home to you, and I was all right. I came in second."

"You're going to have to do better than that if you want to be the regional champ again," she teased him, entranced by the tender expression in his eyes.

"I don't want to be regional champ," he told her. "Brenna, I know what I want. Hear me out," he said as she opened her mouth to protest. "I found some backers and I'm going to start building race cars. And Jeff called me. I start at the community center in the fall." He put his hands on her shoulders, his thumbs beginning an urgent caress. "Brenna, I need you. I love you so much, you're all I can think of, all I thought of the last ten years. I want to marry you. And I want to do it right this time." From under his poncho he produced a black silk tie and held it out toward her. "See? Your father's lucky marrying tie."

Brenna couldn't say anything, just threw herself into his arms, hugging him tightly and feeling his hands rove over her in return. When she could trust her voice, she pulled away until she could see his face, and then she whispered that they were going to have a baby.

His expression was something she would cherish for the rest of her life. It was filled with love, pride, profound awe. "Are you all right?" he murmured, his voice breaking.

Brenna nodded. "I'm scared, but I'm okay as long as you're with me." And she knew it was true. They were going to be all right this time.

Epilogue

"I don't care if you think it's never too early to introduce fiber into the diet, Fergie," Brenna said patiently but firmly. "I'm *not* putting bran on top of my son's first birthday cake."

Clearly offended, Fergie shook his head at Brenna's lack of nutritional savvy. She hid her smile and put the finishing touches on the giant three-layer chocolate cake sitting on the counter of the café. "Did you remember to get extra hamburger buns?" she asked. "Everybody's going to get here any minute."

"Yes, ma'am," Fergie said, still aggrieved.

Brenna took a quick, satisfied look around—at the festive blue-and-white crepe paper, the birthday paper plates and napkins on the table and the cake with its toy car on top. For some reason, no doubt genetic, her son was crazy about cars.

The bell over the door rang and Brenna looked up, smiling broadly when Luke walked in, their son, one year old today, in his arms. "Happy birthday, sweet James," Brenna said, laughing in pure pleasure just at the sight of him. James, named for Luke's father, grinned back and held out his arms to her. "Such a happy baby," Brenna murmured to him, and it was true. Her child was a perpetual smiler, and he seemed to have inherited his father's charm, as well.

"Hi, honey," Brenna said, kissing Luke over James's head.

Spying one of the many toy cars kept around the café expressly for his amusement, James grinned and pointed. Brenna set him on the floor, watching proudly as he toddled toward the chair where the car sat, his chubby hands flopping high in the air for balance. When Brenna looked up she found Luke watching her with the same expression she suspected was on her own face. It still filled them with awe to think they could ever be this happy. The days of pain and loneliness had largely faded into memory, and life was abundantly good to them.

"I took your car by Avery's to get new tires put on," Luke said, pulling Brenna close to him and rubbing his chin against her hair.

"I'm not sure I want to hear this," Brenna said, and Luke leaned back to give her a grin. "It looks like the brakes need replacing, too." He gave her a teasing raise of the eyebrows. "You want to sell the car?"

"Heck, no!" Brenna retorted. "I figure that car is some kind of test from God."

Luke laughed and was on the verge of pulling her close again when the door opened and people began arriving for James's birthday party.

An hour later Brenna was knee-deep in presents and cards and the hamburgers Fergie was doling out on paper plates. Luke walked past her with a bowl of potato chips and stopped long enough to nibble on her ear.

"No smooching with the cook!" Brenna's father called out from his table, James on his lap. Luke grinned.

"*I'm* the cook," Fergie advised him with narrowed eyes. "And ain't nobody smooching with me."

Luke returned from the kitchen and stood beside Brenna, slipping his arm around her waist. She surveyed the scene and felt a pleasure so deep that it seemed rooted in her soul.

Her dad was helping James play with his race car on the tabletop, Jason Conley and his brothers were listening to Fergie expound on the virtues of oat bran, Loraine was advising Avery, Denny and Julie that a fool and his money made hay while the sun shone, and Waldo's intrepid insurance agent, Frank Hargrove, was doubtfully telling Cloris and Thaddeus Hennesy that he wasn't rightly sure he could insure them against alien brainwashing.

All in all, life was good at the Chestnut Tree Cafe.

*   *   *   *   *

Back by popular demand, some of Diana Palmer's earliest published books are available again!

Several years ago, Diana Palmer began her writing career. Sweet, compelling and totally unforgettable, these are the love stories that enchanted readers everywhere.

Next month, six more of these wonderful stories will be available in DIANA PALMER DUETS—Books 4, 5 and 6. Each DUET contains two powerful stories plus an introduction by Diana Palmer. Don't miss:

Book Four	AFTER THE MUSIC DREAM'S END
Book Five	BOUND BY A PROMISE PASSION FLOWER
Book Six	TO HAVE AND TO HOLD THE COWBOY AND THE LADY

SILHOUETTE'S "BIG WIN"
SWEEPSTAKES RULES & REGULATIONS
NO PURCHASE NECESSARY TO ENTER OR RECEIVE A PRIZE

A duo by Laurie Paige

There's no place like home—and Laurie Paige's delightful duo captures the heartwarming feeling in two special stories set in Arizona ranchland. Share the poignant homecomings of two lovely heroines—half sisters Lainie and Tess— as they travel on the road to romance with their rugged, handsome heroes.

A SEASON FOR HOMECOMING—Lainie and Dev's story...available in June

HOME FIRES BURNING BRIGHT—Tess and Carson's story...available now

Come home to A SEASON FOR HOMECOMING (#727) and HOME FIRES BURNING BRIGHT (#733) . . . only from Silhouette Romance!

Diana Palmer's fortieth story for Silhouette ... chosen as an Award of Excellence title!

CONNAL
Diana Palmer

Next month, Diana Palmer's bestselling LONG, TALL TEXANS series continues with CONNAL. The skies get cloudy on C. C. Tremayne's home on the range when Penelope Mathews decides to protect him—by marrying him!

One specially selected title receives the Award of Excellence every month. Look for CONNAL in August at your favorite retail outlet ... only from Silhouette Romance.

CON-1

Diamond Jubilee Collection

It's our 10th Anniversary... and *you* get a present!

This collection of early Silhouette Romances features novels written by three of your favorite authors:

ANN MAJOR—*Wild Lady*
ANNETTE BROADRICK—*Circumstantial Evidence*
DIXIE BROWNING—*Island on the Hill*

* These Silhouette Romance titles were first published in the early 1980s and have not been available since!

* Beautiful Collector's Edition bound in antique green simulated leather to last a lifetime!

* Embossed in gold on the cover and spine!

This special collection will not be sold in retail stores and is only available through this exclusive offer.
Look for details in all Silhouette series published in June, July and August.